THE CHEERLE

AND OTHER TALES

By the Same Author in Notion Press

Laugh and Let Laugh

THE CHEERLESS CHAUFFEUR AND OTHER TALES

CHINMAY CHAKRAVARTY

INDIA · SINGAPORE · MALAYSIA

Notion Press

No. 8, 3rd Cross Street,
CIT Colony, Mylapore,
Chennai, Tamil Nadu – 600 004

First Published by Notion Press 2021
Copyright © Chinmay Chakravarty 2021
All Rights Reserved.

ISBN 978-1-63781-691-2

In Loving Memory of
my more of a kid brother than a brother-in-law,
Dr. Aswini Kumar Sarma (1961–2020),
who left for the heavenly abode
so early and suddenly, leaving us shattered…

CONTENTS

1. A Civilization 9

2. Framed 13

3. Pinned Down 17

4. The Banana Breakout 20

5. The Viral Veto! 24

6. An Elaborate Concoction 28

7. Tales, Telltales and Tailspin 31

8. The Connecting Train 36

9. Less Order on the Superfast Express 40

10. Brown Sugar and the Olden Rage 45

11. 'Well Done, Senor!' 48

12. The Loner! 50

13. Two Strangers at It 56

14. The Haunted Pajama! 58

15. The Burpy Blues 62

16. A Punch in the Lurch 65

17. The Peculiar Mystery of a Parcel 68

18. The Cheerless Chauffeur 72

19.   The Rain Drench! 78

20.   The Munching Ways of a Miser 83

21.   A Bluff of the Hazardous Kind..............................88

22.   The Spit-Fire..94

23.   Milord…O' Landlord 98

24.   "You Are Invited…!" (1)....................................100

25.   "You Are Invited…!" (2)....................................103

26.   The Duel..107

27.   Out of the Clue...109

28.   A Curious Case for Delays..................................114

29.   "Because I Needed to Buy…!" 117

30.   The Rough Cut! 121

31.   The Discerning Commuter 125

32.   The Decibels of Desperation 128

33.   The Bloated Musician 133

34.   The Thames Pond Quadrilogy 136

      1. Credit Control Room..............................136

      2. The Cost of Credit..................................139

      3. Cash on the Cards 141

      4. The Virtual Travel Package 144

A CIVILIZATION

He just looks majestic, tall, fair, of lithe build and wavy black hair. He has sharp features; his eyes shine through his myopic glasses; he has a hook-billed nose and a baritone—soft-spoken, however. His dress code is always perfect for the occasion. He is also a teetotaler and a non-smoker, to the best of my understanding. His name is Nandan Gupta. He lives in a fourth-floor apartment in the suburbs of a big city in India. He retired from a middle-level executive post in a private company four years back. For me, he is like an embodiment of our civilization. The finest specimen I've ever met in my thirty-odd lifetime, I decide.

CR80

I made his acquaintance quite accidentally. He came to our news agency office with a query about a particular item published in local newspapers. Gupta impressed me at the very first sight, and our conversation brought us closer, instantly, despite our age difference. He too seemed to like me a lot and invited me to his home, surely not an empty gesture because he gave me his residential address. In the following days, we regularly talked over the phone; he reminded me of his invitation every time.

So, on a free evening, I visited him. The building, constructed perhaps decades back, had no lift. A little out of breath after reaching the fourth floor, I pressed the doorbell. Gupta himself opened the door and heartily welcomed me in. As he made me sit on the velvety sofa, I took a look around. It was a huge rectangular living room dressed up with taste and class.

In between our conversation, he said proudly, "…thank God for giving me a good life. I enjoy life fully…enjoy the good of everything. And of course, I love comforts. Don't you think I deserve it? I worked hard for this…!"

Another evening, he mused aloud, "You see…in my prime, the left ideology attracted me a lot. But when I met their leaders discussing poverty with glasses of expensive wine in air-conditioned rooms…well, I left the 'left'…!"

On my every visit, his wife, also tall, slim and of a striking appearance, joined us for some time and then used to serve us the customary tea-biscuits.

However, returning home, I couldn't help but wonder often: *Why does his wife wear a constant scowl on her face? Why do our sessions never extend into supper even when I get quite late in leaving?* I had no answers, and so I used to dismiss the thoughts as trivial. Sometimes he said to me with a wink, "I'd soon visit your bachelorhood house…will taste how good you cook…!"

CRSO

One morning, he called me up saying there was going to be a big classical music event that evening and he had two passes. "My wife is indisposed. I hope you'd not mind accompanying me," he continued without waiting for my affirmation. "So, we'll meet at a common place somewhere. OK?"

I agreed. I was always fond of Indian classical music concerts and never wanted to miss an opportunity.

We met at the appointed place and proceeded to the auditorium at the elite southernmost part of the city. We were given two good seats in the second row.

Midway, the stage anchor announced an interval, and that tea-snacks were to be served to all at the lounge, free of cost. To my surprise, Gupta stood up immediately. "Come…come! Let's rush…!" he cried.

There was already a big queue outside. Gupta looked very annoyed. "See those dirty-rich people in dirty-costly apparels…waiting for the freebies! They'll spend thousands at the five-star restaurants…and yet won't ever miss anything free! Shameless…!"

By the time we reached the counter, one of the attendants put up two steaming cups of tea for us. "Give us the hot snack you're distributing!" Gupta ordered.

"Sorry, Sir! We ran out of stock…please do not mind!"

"What the hell do you mean 'ran out of stock'?" thundered Gupta. "You know exactly how many passes were given out. You must arrange…I won't accept…take it away!"

I stood there, looking at him in amazement. I came to my senses quickly though. He was already attracting a lot of attention, and there were many people still left in the queue. I picked up the two cups and somehow managed to take him to a corner of the lounge.

I tried my best to calm him down, but he continued to grumble. He grimaced at every sip he took.

I couldn't concentrate on the post-interval session; I was perturbed and confused.

After it was over, Gupta exclaimed, "My bachelor friend, let's rush to a good joint! I'm ravenously hungry!"

In fact, he took me to his favorite restaurant; an expensive one too. As we entered, the milling waiters smiled warmly at Gupta and took us to a table in a cozy corner. Gupta started ordering—beers, starters, main course, ice-cream. I felt distinctly uneasy looking at the price column of the menu. I tried to tell him that I had kept my supper ready at home, but could only stammer.

He ignored me; greedily drank and ate, talking incessantly. A chilling presentiment grew stronger within me.

Finishing our meal, out of the corner of my eye, I saw a waiter approaching our table with the bill book. He came up, and to my horror, politely presented the bill to me. *My Goodness! They know him very well here…a regular customer…then why the heck…!* I wondered silently, in pain.

At the same time, Nandan Gupta excused himself to the restroom, leaving me alone with my plight…

ॐ

I reach home, undress, get refreshed and lie down on my bed, wondering about Nandan Gupta all the while. I try fending off a scowl that threatens to distort my countenance. *The finest specimen…!* I mumble to myself as a dry laugh croaks out of my throat. I sink my head deep into the pillows, and go to sleep instantly.

FRAMED

Kamal finalized the schedule of going for the evening show directly from the office. He could not afford to miss it. The actor-director had been known to him, on the silver screen only, for quite a long time, and she was famous for making artistic and serious movies, both in Hindi and in an Indian regional language. He had watched most of her films since his college days, and always enjoyed those.

Today's was a special screening of her latest Hindi film, a kind of a premiere show perhaps, few days before the theatrical release. Kamal knew that serious films like this one never merited a glamorous premiere or a commercial release, and therefore, such special screenings were a boon for the discerning moviegoers. He was particularly happy with the fact that the filmmaker would be present there in person. His entry pass was for two. His wife of two years of wedlock earlier expressed her inability to go for it that particular day. So, he requested his best friend-colleague to accompany him. The friend agreed, but due to a last-minute engagement, he finally expressed his regrets too.

Kamal did not quite mind going alone because such thought-provoking films had better be enjoyed alone. He wanted to leave the office early but got a bit delayed due to an important visitor who came late. Finally, free, he rushed out to the bus stop and was grateful to get it immediately. *Even if the bus takes half an hour in this peak-traffic hour, I should be on time for the show,* he thought. And he did reach the sprawling auditorium complex on time.

As was natural for serious movies, the show was arranged in the mini auditorium on the ground floor. Without bothering to look at the people still sipping tea and talking in the lounge, Kamal went in straight away and was gratified to get a very good seat in the rear. The show started on time after a brief intro by the actor-director. He thoroughly enjoyed watching. More so, because there was no interval as the film was around one and half-hour's duration only. After the movie ended, he continued to sit for some time, thinking about it and relishing the precious moments of the movie. Finally, he came out fully satisfied and with a rather misty pair of eyes.

He saw several groups of people engaged in animated discussion in the lounge, sparklingly well-lit now. He pondered for a moment about taking a cup of tea from the busy counter. But, he mused, *Why spend so much whereas I'll get a better-made cup of tea in the roadside stall outside at a fraction of the price here!* As he moved toward the exit, he suddenly caught sight of the actor-director surrounded by a much larger group. She looked beautiful and heavenly under the lights despite being in her fifties, and Kamal discovered a resolve evolving fast within him.

Yes, he always wanted to meet her. He had so many things to discuss and tell her, and so much appreciation to convey to her. About today's movie, in particular, he wanted to congratulate her and wanted eagerly to tell her his opinion, already formed delicately in his cinema-appreciation mold. With the resolve firm within him, Kamal started loitering around closing in on that target group. Finally, reaching a conveniently nearer spot, he took two firm steps toward her and froze. *She was staring at him with intent and an unwavering gaze.*

Normally, such a stare from a very important lady would have pleased him immensely. But something in the stare disturbed him and effected an unpleasant churning in him. She was looking at him as if she were going to devour him right there and then. Kamal seemed to perceive although not very sure about that—that there was some sort of an abominable carnality in the gaze. He got scared. An overwhelming premonition of danger engulfed him. Kamal took another decisive resolve.

He bolted out of the lounge, and almost ran to the bus stop. Again gratified, he got it quickly and got a window seat too. And his mind raced: *Was I right about the stare? Has my feeling about her look reflected her feelings about me?* He was not very sure. However, he mused on: *Gut feelings are mostly right and should always be adhered to, respected. I must have done the right thing.* As the bus raced toward the local railway station where he would get a direct train home, three options to the issue at hand shaped up in his mind.

First, his gut feelings were genuine. Second, she could have been interested in him from the filmy point of view, that is to say, possibly casting him in her future projects. And third, both options are right. Now, Kamal embarked on a cost-benefit analysis.

Option 1: He does the right thing...the innocent face of his wife fading in and out constantly. *She is indeed carnivorous or omnivorous or whatever, or cadaverous? Shit, that is the wrong word! Firm conclusion,* he escaped.

Option 2: Here he must have missed an opportunity; he does not boast of being young and handsome, people, particularly from the fairer variety, say this. *Firm conclusion,* he lost out sorely.

Option 3: She is interested in him both from the *carnality* angle and the *casting* possibility; he must have won here too... *Yes...wife's innocent face...yes...lost an opportunity... no...wife...break...no...yes. Firm conclusion, not firm at all; damn it all!*

PINNED DOWN

He was at a total loss to understand how he could be so dumb and stupid. He felt ashamed of himself, a manager at an insurance company, recalling the memory of it, although it had been only a few weeks ago. He somehow took solace in the fact that perhaps the helpline executive he phoned was the dumbest, stupidest, abysmal nincompoop at best! On his own stupidity, he often tried to justify it—the unending months of stay-at-home and work-from-home on account of the pandemic perhaps made him a fool-proof digital being, concerned only with streams of passwords, PINs and IDs. But the fact remained; he was really stupid, he pondered pensively.

Actually, his old mobile phone was giving him constant trouble from the beginning of the lockdown. It had given hangs, sudden shutdowns, blank screens and problems with the operating system. There was no way of getting it repaired any time soon. It was a huge setback for him given the demanding virtual times. He had no option but to wait. After about two months of lockdown, for the first time, e-commerce of non-essentials was allowed temporarily. He grabbed the opportunity and booked a rather costly smartphone online; he needed a powerful camera, more storage capacity and more speed.

Luckily, the smartphone was delivered in real quick time. Ecstatically, he opened the package and took the elegant device in his hands. He wanted to get it working immediately. He took out the SIM card from his old phone, and thence the trouble began.

He failed to find the usual opening on the backside for putting in the card. Fiddling with it for quite some time and yet failing to find the SIM card slot, he rummaged through the package checking the accessories and the guide booklet. He howled in anger, finding the guide too brief, giving no indication about inserting SIM cards. He wanted to call his wife, but she was too busy in the kitchen at the time.

Even though he hated doing it, he looked for the service center helpline number and dialed. He was finally directed to a customer service executive.

"Good morning! How can I help you, Sir?"

He told him about the problem.

"I'm sorry for the inconvenience. Sir, please check the package. You'll find the pin there."

"I searched many times, but no PIN is given."

"But, Sir, the pin is always provided along with the set."

"I told you it's not there. And how is it possible? I've bought a brand-new set; every facility has to be provided. Tell me again, is it written somewhere in the backside of the model?"

"No, Sir! It's provided with the accessories."

"But it's not there! How to start my phone now?"

"You'll have to visit our nearest service center; only they can provide the pin."

"What do you mean? How the hell I am supposed to go there? You know the situation! Horrible service! I'm sorry I went for your model!" he bellowed now.

"Extremely sorry for the inconvenience, Sir! Please…!"

The enraged 'customer' cut the line.

His wife entered the scene now hearing the commotion. He answered her queries rather reluctantly, his ego against expressing his absolute helplessness.

His wife took the instrument in her hands and produced a safety pin as if out of thin air. She unclasped the sharp pin and inserted it into a tiny hole on one side of the mobile. And lo! Out came the SIM card tray! She asked for the SIM; he gave it to her readily. She fitted it carefully in one slot and pushed the tray in. And the smartphone started working immediately. She handed him the phone back and exited the scene with a triumphant smile.

He cursed the executive for not telling him the obvious: that the PIN was in fact a mere pin, which he could have extracted very easily from his office files. However, one question remained in his mind, *Even if the mere pin was, in fact, a PIN, how the hell would I have applied it on a dead damned instrument?*

Anyway, he thought over it again: *Who is the bigger fool? In my defense, I have the fact that I've not been used to costly smartphones with ejecting SIM card trays! So, what about the executive? Well, the poor fellow probably had no clue about his customer's colossal ignorance!*

THE BANANA BREAKOUT

She lost her temper very often nowadays. *Not at all surprising under the present circumstances,* Nandini reasoned. Her life had been reduced to a saga of non-stop drudgery—from early morning to late night, without a break till she falls like a log on the double bed more than half of which is always occupied by Barun, her husband. Well, she did not mind work. She had always been an active and agile person who preferred to remain busy; she in fact hated idleness. However, in this case, she was getting mercilessly deprived of her privacy—her private moments were always important in her life. Nandini found herself unable to wave off the strong sense of nostalgia. *Nostalgia? What the hell!* It had been just four months earlier when her life was going on the usual way.

Since her marriage about twenty years back, she had been getting used to a set daily routine. She would rise early from bed, make tea and the meals, send off Barun to the office with the ever-present tiffin box, have her breakfast, and then would welcome the maid in for the domestic clean-up while chatting with her carefree and relaxed. After the maid left, she would have the rest of the day to herself for relaxing, making phone calls to parents or relatives or her friends until her husband joined around seven in the evening—every day, except for holidays and Sundays, when the time spent together or the outings seemed heavenly. The arrival of the children, first the daughter after two years of marriage, and then the son with a two-year gap, made her routing only tighter, but still giving her the private moments she was always so fond of. She was a Bachelor's degree holder, but never really wanted a job, taking care of her household being the most important assignment. And that had been the story of her life as a housewife until four months ago.

Now everything had changed. Every single member of the household would stay put at home: the children would occupy most of the hall of Nandini's one-bedroom-hall-kitchen flat with their smartphones often requiring absolute quiet for their online classes; Barun would sprawl on the bed watching television news as if he were the only one on earth needing to be abreast of happenings the world over, and the maid would not come. Nandini would remain confined mostly to her humid-hot kitchen cooking. She was surprised that all of them seemed to be ravenously hungry at all times despite the long idleness, and worse, they'd want newer and newer dishes to be prepared. The nature of Barun's work made work-from-home minimal and whenever he sat down before his desktop in the bedroom, he would complain more of the Wi-Fi internet service being monopolized by the children than work.

At first, Nandini took her routine as a natural new normal, but slowly and steadily, got bored and impatient. How could she just go on like this: rise early morning to clean the house before everyone else woke up; then prepare the breakfast—first for her children and then for Barun who rose from bed in an infuriatingly leisurely way; then she would start preparing for lunch—not able to combine cooking for the night too as the exquisite connoisseurs did not want stale food for any meal; she'd hardly manage a catnap as the chattering of the late-rising Barun never ceased; then, time for the evening tea for all preferably with a hot snack and by the time she felt a little free, it was time for preparing dinner, and when finally past midnight she'd fall flat on the bed like a log, the television would still go on.

All essentials came home, that is to say, at the lobby of the society from where these were to be collected, which Barun did generously—from online booking or from the local grocery store orders. She'd often encourage Barun to go out for fresh vegetables and fruits from the vendors who served till about seven in the evening. But he would not budge: he considered himself as the elderly although he was not yet fifty and so would not take any risk. For that very purpose, he barred the children too from going out.

Over the weeks, the suffocation became unbearable for Nandini and she was really desperate now. Petty quarrels with her husband started becoming violent, eliciting tremendous disapproval and ire from the children. And then she hit upon an idea. It was true that she found the bananas delivered online not at all fresh that hardly lasted two days as each of them gobbled up two or three bananas every morning. She tried with her banana-centrist idea and said to Barun:

"Look, Barun! This continuous stay-at-home without some physical activity is not good for you. It'll slowly decrease your immunity and finally, when everything becomes normal, you'll be most likely to get infected the moment you go out. These are not my words, but experts', you know. You must do something to increase your immunity. I'm never free, dancing around the house most part of the day and so I don't need to exercise…see, now evening walks are allowed, and you can see how bad the bananas are. You all love bananas! So, go out in the evening, take a stroll, sit in the garden and buy fresh bananas from the local vendor—only a little away from our society complex. Please…!"

It worked to her great relief. Every alternate day gave her the much-needed free moments on the bed—gratefully alone and private. It didn't matter for how long—just fifteen minutes of privacy did wonders for her distressed self. Of course, she never ceased thanking God for keeping them safe and relatively better-off from many others because Barun had his monthly salary still ensured. Nandini, a classical homemaker, wished well for all in her family and for all of the whole country and the world…

THE VIRAL VETO!

It seemed like a conquest for Umashankar. For the first time after months of continuous stay-at-home, he had ventured out; he had taken this momentous decision considering the utmost necessity of some natural physical movement apart from the arbitrary jumps and jerks he indulged in at home every morning; he had to ensure that he was still a normal man.

The infections rose ominously recently and in view of that, the restrictions were intensified, not allowing strolls and jogs even within the housing society campus. For a senior person like him, stay-at-home was more severely enforced, both by the society and the members of his family. But he had to feel normal, he decided. So, one afternoon, when his wife and daughter-in-law were taking a nap, his son out on emergency office work and his grandson busy with his online classes, he ventured out, taking the house keys along.

He felt a bit apprehensive approaching the main gate, but the security guards only stared at him, not saying or questioning anything. Once out of the campus and hitting the lane, he was free and enthralled. To make it better, the patrolling cops were also not in sight. Yes, the world did not change permanently in the meanwhile, with more cars, tempos and cabs plying now. Of course, pedestrians were conspicuously less in number and, persons of his age were a rarity. He started walking briskly swinging his hands and flexing his muscles.

In a few minutes, Umashankar reached the grocery supermarket, a place he visited so often with his wife or his daughter-in-law, in the normal times. He stopped, feeling tempted to go in and shop as usual. People were going in and coming out; some loading their cars with the rations purchased; some crowding around the staff-desk outside for the compulsory hand-sanitization and thermal check, and some members of staff hurrying here and there, checking and supervising. He killed his temptation. No, he could not afford that. Many of the recent infections were traced back to the store and, he, being a senior citizen, had to show his love and gratification for his family's responsible actions.

He looked around and decided to cross the highway. On the other side, most of the shops were open. Walking along a service road, he noticed that his favorite restaurant was also open. The manager sat relaxed, yawning behind the counter, and a few of the waiters adorned the doorway looking at him hopefully. He stopped, feeling tempted again: he wanted to just occupy one of the tables arranged seductively and sparingly too, and order one of his favorite dishes to be packed. No, he could not afford this, for the same reasons, and one more—the virus was believed to last longer on plastic packets. He started walking again. At the crossroads, he turned left to the main arterial road, which led to the busiest market area.

A few stores of various kinds were open only on one side of the road, and the vegetable-fish-meat market was closed. He saw a tiny tea-stall managed by an old woman open with no sippers around. He felt the urge of having that pleasure again. *Ah! This simple indulgence now seems like a sought-after luxury.* The tea-stall triggered in him a much stronger urge. Ah! How desperately he wanted to have that indulgence in the open air again, sans the mask. However, to his disappointment or relief, not sure which, those kinds of small shops were still closed, or more correctly, still not allowed to do business. He turned his attention to a stationery store that he frequented, and again felt tempted to do some minimal shopping. *No to all,* he muttered sternly. He walked on taking the circular road back toward the highway.

As he waited for the signal to turn green at the highway crossing, he observed that the traffic looked almost normal. A half-empty city bus came to its customary halt at the stop just on his left, and he felt tempted again to jump in and indulge in that pleasure so sorely missed in the last few months. *Further,* he thought, *the malls were allowed to do business now with strict norms, and so, why not visit the nearest one, only for a change, if not for shopping?* Immediately, Umashankar killed that lure too, for the same or similar reasons.

Umashankar started feeling scared: how his now-proven fickle mind had been rather cruelly exposing him to all sorts of impulses, desires and temptations, making him more vulnerable than even his age can do. The moment the signal turned green, he crossed over hurriedly in a half-run and started walking back home. The security guard just looked at him, with utter indifference that got further heightened by a yawn.

Reaching his floor, Umashankar quietly inserted the house key and opened the door. His grandson, watching television now, looked up at him ominously. He gave the kid a benevolent smile saying that he just had a look around in the campus. Luckily for Umashankar, the grandson found the television movie much more interesting than the supposed surreptitious behavior of an old man. As he sat down contentedly on the sofa, Umashankar felt happy that the daring outing had granted him at least a good opportunity for a feeling of normalcy, even though momentarily.

AN ELABORATE CONCOCTION

The ecstasy threatened to spill over his mouth, lips, teeth and eyes. He considered it wise to suppress his feelings. *The time is just not right,* he reasoned. *One should not look or sound too happy.* The last few days, he had been extremely irritable, depressed and angry. He felt deprived, poor and powerless—to the extent that his deprivation made him rather depraved. He couldn't find joy in anything: in the homemade dishes presented to him, in making petty conversations with the members of the family, all sitting at home for days, in the occasional errands for him, in watching the television news or surfing the smartphones and so on.

Every day, he went out with his car—apart from the regular visits to the grocery stores, the vegetable and fruit shops—and mostly roamed around the city's near-empty roads looking for his valuable acquaintances in key trades, and trying to convince whomsoever he managed to catch up with the hopeless situation. However, they too expressed their helplessness; nothing was possible as the rules were absolutely strict. Coming back home in a devastated state of mind, he often complained bitterly to his father, a former top bureaucrat who still exercised enough clout in the administration, about the mindless clampdown. He could also see his father's state of increasing agitation and restlessness. He reassured himself; his father was trying his best, only not managing to convince the people in power so far.

"Look at the two members of one family alone, and examine what a mess they are being reduced to," he murmured contemptuously, "then, you bring into the picture all other persons who must have fallen ill or are about to crash by now due to such unreasonable decisions! And they consider these as non-essential items! Damn them all!" He did not however give up all hope: he had great faith in his father who always showered him with all privileges and favors of high influencing society—that even now he was moving freely with the car despite the heavy restrictions and the numerous checkpoints.

And suddenly, the relaxation was announced late one evening: the shops would reopen from the next day, and all customers were asked to queue up observing social distancing strictly. He started making his plans immediately.

Early morning the next day, he parked his car at quite a distance from the shop: he never wanted himself to be seen languishing in the queue by his relatives and some friends whom he referred to as 'goody-goody fools'. He made an elaborate plan: arranging ten errand-boys of various ages, asking them to join the queue at different times, observe discipline and social distancing and giving each of them the required money including tips. Drumming his fingers over the steering wheel, he waited—in ecstatic expectation.

One by one, the ten delivery boys started coming up to the car with plastic packets. As one came, he would open the door and ask him to keep the packet neatly on the rear seat. Presently, all ten packets were delivered—kept safely behind him. The slight tinkling emanating from the packets sounded the sweetest and heavenly for him. Thanking his father silently as ever, he drove with gay abandon occasionally waving at the policemen managing a checkpoint and being waved back.

"But no," he sermonized himself, "you must not get carried away. We must enforce rational rationing because the lockdown is being extended—not sure for how many more days. The shops could get closed again too." The upcoming session with his father beckoned to him lovingly, rather intoxicating him already.

TALES, TELLTALES AND TAILSPIN

He was facing an existential crisis: should he stop watching news television forthwith or continue watching at his own peril? He was not able to decide the best course of action. Some of his friends, why his own wife, too, on many occasions, had been advising him to strictly not watch news channels. Because, they opined, it had been very negative with everything, and, essentially, why should one go on being a mute witness to the reports of how many millions had been infected with the virus and how many thousands had succumbed to it? It affects you in the wrong way, makes you despondent and depressed, they added most emphatically. But, how could he just give up on news? He had to keep up with the local, national and the world scenario for his information, understanding and possibly analysis, particularly in this pandemic situation. And what were the alternatives? He did not still get his newspapers, and he quickly got tired of reading e-papers. His mind went into a spin.

Some friends had even put up social media posts, proudly informing others that they had stopped watching news channels. He got disturbed. He reasoned: all of the channels are not that loud and that bad, and for a change, they do show some extremely important content; he was intellectually smart enough to decipher the news from the views inherent in it; and like in a buffet party, he could choose and pick the items he needed. Yes, he had already discarded the channels with the towering lunatics with their even more demonic companions. He had been sticking to this new normal, with a self-conscious pride of sorts, until those tales surfaced with their telltale signs, and left him flabbergasted, gasping for a breath of clarity or solace.

He was perplexed, veritably, genuinely. *Why have the news channels suddenly switched on to the tales of two lovely ladies, at a time when the virus has been surging and spiking record-highs of infections and deaths all across his miserable country? Perhaps,* he reasoned, *they too wanted a change from the depressing scenario, and perhaps wanted to earn a few bucks more, by arranging delicious on-sale dishes on the buffet.* He was still perplexed as well as angry: all the lessons, tips and insights he had learned from the channels had almost gone waste because the same preaching channels had shown how desperate they were for the two lovely ladies, negating themselves in the observance of all norms of social distancing in their mad rush to take in whatever came out of them, in full glory and in exhaustively breaking details. He, an honest person basically, was disgusted with the near media-riots that kept on being created day after day as the tales and telltales of the lovely ladies unfolded.

His depth of perplexity increased further, trying to make his personal stands clear as to the intricate stories of the two actors. He respected and adored them both: the first one as the caring girlfriend of the dead actor, a rising star, whom he loved, too, on the big screen; the second one he had always loved to watch on the big screens, particularly for her portrayals in her off-beat movies. Now, in their real-life acts, he could not decide who to support, oppose or hate.

The first case confounded him. He failed to understand why at all the dead actor's family in his source state decided to complain against the girlfriend after nearly a month of his tragic but apparent suicide in the target state. However, what followed interested him more.

The ruling dispensation of the source state had thrown itself overwhelmingly in support of the family, making it, arguably, the most powerful on earth, apart from perhaps the dynastic ones. The news channels, discarded by him, also came in with servile cacophonous support, and the accuser-in-chief and the towering lunatic of a particular channel started his investigations, and convicted the poor girl before anybody, with his derisive followers clapping in hyena-like ecstasy. After a series of confrontations, cross accusations and court verdicts, the three main investigating agencies started their operations, displaying an unprecedented hurry. Her final arrest was hailed as a vindication by all in support and condemned as vindictive by all opposed. The problem for him was that he respected the investigating agencies, too, from his years of existential experience in his miserable country, and he was unable to decide who was guilty, actually.

Before the news channels got a breather from the first case, the second lady burst into the scene, without much foreplay. She willfully accused the people and the government of the target state, where she herself lived and earned, of unspeakable things, even comparing it to an eternal enemy-nation. The abominable things she uttered should have, ideally, hurt the feelings of both the ruling dispensations of the target state and the other stakeholders across the miserable country. However, while the ruling dispensation of the target state reacted vehemently, coming out, as expected by the main stakeholders, with its knee-jerk 'punishment' measures, the main stakeholders decided to provide to the lady maximum possible security for an actor ever. The sheer violation of norms that followed at the airport where both supporters and opposers and, of course, the media-persons assembled in huge numbers for the arrival of the actor, made him boiling angry. The news channels, discarded by him, made the din worse by announcing the loudest of support for the lovely lady and crying for the blood of the authorities of the target state.

Two ladies: one continuously hounded and finally jailed, for her guilt yet to be proved conclusively; and the other lady who said disgustingly unparliamentary things was made a hero. Of course, he was not so naïve and gullible. As for the 'hounding' case, he saw clearly that the ruling dispensation of the source state had indisputable electoral gains to make from its 'son of soil' dead actor, and the main stakeholder had a revenge angle on the target state where it had suffered a great betrayal by its traditional partner. As for the 'hailing' case, he could see that the main stakeholder stood to make strong headway into exacting revenge in the target state. In any case, the two lovely ladies continued to haunt him.

However, his basic existential crisis was yet to be solved: to continue or stop watching news television. Well, there was no hurry, at least in his own case. In the meantime, he could continue with his new normal adaptation, except for the occasional sneak-ins in the discarded channels just for curiosity, as he normally indulged in. But he was sure about one thing: the news channels, along with their governments, must put the focus back on the real raging crisis. And his final decision would rest squarely on this.

THE CONNECTING TRAIN

I was supremely confident that the connecting train would wait for us. Our first train was running five hours late, and the onward connecting train was to leave from the big junction about three hours after the scheduled arrival of our train. Most of the passengers booked for that train had given up hope. I tried my best to infuse confidence in them by pointing out the obvious fact that our reservation tickets showed confirmed births on the connecting train, and therefore, it was a sacred obligation on the part of the Indian Railways to make the train wait for us. Some of the depressed co-passengers believed in me. I was not only mistaken but was colossally being naive.

Yes, the connecting train left at the scheduled departure time, more than two hours before our final arrival, leaving us stranded for the night at the station waiting room. Of course, the ticket was valid and it was adjusted in the train leaving early the next morning for our destination. This was the first case of missing the connecting train, and it was by a huge margin.

The next time, we boarded the same train to connect at the big junction for our onward journey; we were much closer to catching it—missing it by just an hour. And the same routine followed at the station for the next early-morning train.

It happened for the third time in a row, and the third time was a real big chase of sorts.

That third time, our train was running two hours late, and so we were very hopeful of catching the connecting train because the time difference was three hours. The nail-biting chase began when we reached a small station about thirty kilometers from the big junction. The train was a little less than two hours late now, and it needed only half an hour more to complete the journey to yield us enough time to board the connecting train. We got busy packing up, feeling elated that finally, we were going to make it on our third attempt.

However, the rail gods had some other plans for us hapless souls. The train, a superfast one, continued to wait at the nondescript station…for minutes…half-hour…and more. We were getting really worried as the buffer time we had was drying out fast and furious. Now we started debating loud and louder with ire and great irritation. Some experienced souls opined that the platform clearance was not given perhaps due to heavy local train traffic or maybe some other issues like goods train movement or derailment. Nothing helped, though, as our irritation gave way to plain simple anger.

Finally, our train started moving with less than half an hour's time margin for the connecting train as far as we were concerned. It made good progress picking up great speed, giving us a renewed lease of hope. We were sure of making it when it reached the multi-track entry point of the big junction. And then, it stopped again for the final clearance.

We started praying, 'Please let the connecting train leave a few minutes late…please…dear rail God!' Perhaps as an answer to our prayers, the train moved again on its final leg. We rushed to the doorway with our luggage anticipating which way the platform would come. We discussed our plan of action: two or three passengers would run immediately for the platform of the connecting train, board it and pull the chain while the rest of us would enter through the rear end with the combined luggage. I was part of the more responsible 'luggage' team.

As we entered the targeted platform, we watched in horror the train leaving the platform, maybe about seven minutes late from its scheduled departure time. However, we saw two passengers of our advanced team managing to hop into a coach. So, we kept moving along the moving train hoping it to stop any moment now. Unfortunately, nothing of that kind happened. The speed of the connecting train kept increasing, making us unable to cope with it, and it just disappeared from our disbelieving eyes. We were left stranded there with more baggage and less passengers for comfort.

We took good care of the luggage, taking turns to sleep on the waiting room floor. Early morning, we boarded the other train as on earlier occasions. At the junction midway on the route, the two passengers without luggage getting no benefit by making it to the connecting train and having to spend long hours at the new station floor joined us. I immediately asked them, 'Why didn't you pull the chain?' They said they pulled all the chains available inside the coach, but none of these worked or perhaps their action was ignored by the railway authorities.

We took a solemn pledge never ever to try that particular pair of trains again. And we did stick to our pledge to this very day. We learned to be shrewd, reasonable and wise—go for any connecting train only when the time gap between the pair is at least 10 hours or more.

LESS ORDER ON
THE SUPERFAST EXPRESS

I was happy to see the train already placed and ready for boarding as I entered the platform that afternoon. I was happier to find my two-tier compartment sparsely populated; a bright-looking young man sat hunched over his smartphone on the lower berth opposite mine and the two upper berths were unoccupied. The two side berths were empty too.

I accosted the young man perfunctorily and sat down on my berth in royal comfort after pushing my handbag under the berth. Normally, I didn't get too talkative with fellow passengers, because most of the time, they disappoint you with their casual time-pass manners and, to make it worse, they always seemed to take advantage of anything at your cost. Therefore, on my train journeys, I mostly keep myself busy with books and phones. Of course, I invariably enjoyed the food on board, and in the night, I liked lying down on the berth with the rhythmic movement lulling me into a good slumber. My gastronomy worked much more efficiently, too, than otherwise.

I felt a little annoyed when the train, supposedly a superfast express, refused to budge an inch at the appointed departure time. My annoyance grew as the minutes ticked by. There was no information or announcement, as usual, and on the platform, I couldn't detect any activity that could possibly delay the departure; it was almost empty with all passengers already on board.

Finally, after half an hour, the train made the familiar screeching sound of movement. I felt angry with that totally unaccounted-for delay of thirty minutes that might, in the final count, result in a late arrival by hours. I wanted to vent my anger with a few words addressed to my only fellow passenger, but he was immersed in surfing on his smartphone and was totally oblivious of the delay or anything; perhaps he had already developed a thick skin to all the antics of the Indian Railways. *A bit prematurely,* I thought wisely. I relaxed now trying to push out the negative thoughts from my mind, and hoping that the train would definitely make up for the lost time.

After one and half hours of non-stop running, the train made a halt at a junction. More passengers, reserved from that station, started boarding. A short and stocky middle-aged man with a horse face, a brief mustache and stubble littering his whole face, his wide forehead making inroads further up the head and dressed in jeans and a t-shirt, entered the coach and occupied the lower side-berth in our compartment.

'This goddamned train is already forty minutes late,' were his first words, giving me the all-too-familiar warning. He had two suitcases and a bag with him. Staring with undisguised greed at the empty spaces around us, he pushed in the two suitcases under each of our lower berths although the space under his own berth was empty. I'll refer to this person as Mr. Negativity or simply N hence.

A tall and lanky student also boarded and sat opposite to N, his reservation being for the upper side-berth. N immediately got into a chat with the student and embarked upon his observations about the superfast express: that the train runs late up to 3–4 hours on every journey in both directions, and how he always suffers. To my growing consternation, he found a ready and attentive audience in the student.

As it was getting dark outside, and as I was getting tired of N's greedy stares and pessimistic forecasts, I drew the curtains across to put him out of sight, if not his constant negative chatter. Just before supper time, N pulled the curtains apart as if he owned the railways, and entered our space. He sat down on the opposite berth, took off his shoes shoving the pair under my berth. Then, I was not at all prepared for what he did next.

He began to undress right in front of me! His t-shirt pulled out, his trousers rolled down and finally taken off, leaving him in his underpants which were, fortunately, of the traditionally long variety. Then he pulled one of the suitcases out from under my berth, opened it and took a perfectly ironed night dress out with utmost care. He put it on with equal care and love. Then he folded his pair of jeans and t-shirt as perfectly as possible and placed those inside the suitcase. Finally, he locked the suitcase, pushed it back again and left our space without even a glance at me or at the young man who was smiling at me now. Of course, N left the curtains apart, and I pulled it across instantly. *My goodness! What an impeccable specimen!* I thought.

The night passed off peacefully though and I had a sound sleep. Just before breakfast time, a tall, fair and handsome gentleman, smartly dressed in a suit and tie and probably in his fifties, was passing by us through the aisle; he stopped and retraced his steps examining the numbers of our compartment, and finally sat down on my berth, smiling sweetly at me. I didn't say anything; at daytime, two people sat on the berth, and I assumed the gentleman must have made his sitting reservation.

Meanwhile, the train was running two hours late and unfortunately, was prolonging it, instead of making up. N was in a winning mood; the student too now was expressing his disappointment loudly. I couldn't help interjecting at times, 'Don't be so pessimistic! The train shall definitely gain time; there are not too many halts ahead.' N gave me a pitying grin.

By evening, the ticket examiner came. We all showed our tickets. Looking at the gentleman's ticket, he muttered his disapproval and the gentleman muttered something back to which the examiner seemed to agree, although unhappily. The handsome gentleman got off at the next station giving me that sweet smile again. I realized now that he had enjoyed the journey with only an ordinary ticket, without any reservation, and I had grave doubt about the exact class of his ticket.

The train arrived at the station immediately preceding my destination. I checked the arrival time and found that the train was bang on right time. Now, it was my turn to be in a winning mood. I deliberately addressed the student sitting opposite N and told him proudly that this superfast express always kept some buffer time, and so, the train would finally arrive at the right time. N looked disinterested, looking out of *his* window, for a change.

I started packing my things up as it would take only an hour now for arrival at my destination. The train entered the town premises, and I moved toward the exit passage with my baggage, not knowing which side the doors would open to the platform.

Suddenly, the train came to a screeching halt at the traffic junction, waiting for the green lights. And, the halt went on and on and on. My knees began to hurt as I was standing in the passage hoping to get down soon. The wait extended to nearly two hours, and when finally it reached, I alighted as a totally disillusioned man.

N got down too, perhaps for a walk on the platform. As he passed me, he gave me a lazy look, his triumph was written large over it. Yes, he had a right to be triumphant; the train would surely arrive at its terminus at least three hours late. I cursed N or rather the negativity syndrome, which is always as frequent as the frequently late-running trains, as I strode up the stairs with my bag thrown around my shoulders.

BROWN SUGAR AND
THE OLDEN RAGE

We had about ten minutes before joining the boarding queue. Although we had a good breakfast at the hotel, the running-around packing, carrying/arranging the baggage and the fairly tedious taxi drive to the airport made us hungry again. The prices on board were exorbitant, which meant we had to remain hungry for at least three hours before we reached our destination—not to mention one more tediously long taxi drive home, I reasoned. Therefore, we decided to have a quick bite, and accordingly, leaving my wife with the bags, I ran to a fast-food stall at the airport lounge.

I ordered two chicken puffs and a cup of tea: cannot pay so much for tea, and so one cup will have to provide the rudimentary sips for the two of us. After taking custody of the puffs and a large paper cup of tea, I looked around for the sugar sachets. I picked up a sachet, tore it up and as I was about to pour it over the cup of tea, I suddenly stopped. The contents that came down looked brown and I found the color suspicious: I thought it could be some kind of spice. I threw the packet away and finding another tray with other sachets, picked up one, and to my satisfaction this time it was white and homely.

I was not aware of a customer standing alongside me. His words addressed to me made me look at him; I found him to be a security or police person as he was in that khaki uniform.

He was saying to me, "Don't throw that. It is brown sugar, and it is very good for you old chaps—very healthy indeed!"

His expression 'old chaps' hit my eardrums with an absolutely adverse impact, and it made me angry instantly. *How dare you call me old!* However, I kept my decency; but I had a point to catch him off-guard, so I cried in feigned surprise.

"Brown sugar! How do you mean?"

"No, no! It is not *that* brown sugar! This, you know, is made of *gud* (jaggery), which is supposed to be very good for people even with diabetes. At your age, you must know about this!"

"Yes, I do know. But I don't like it with tea, I like the *rosogollas* made with *gud*, no doubt!" I neatly collected my precious items and left in a hurry—more to avoid speaking again to that 'insulting' personage than for the time constraint. As I was walking away with long strides, I could still hear him commenting on various other sweets made with *gud*.

I re-joined my wife with a grave expression on my face, but this apparent oddity at that hour escaped her attention altogether as she was busy talking on her mobile.

The serpentine queue at the boarding gate was already formed, and so we started attacking the puffs furiously while indulging occasionally in the limited sips available with the tea. All the while on this act, I couldn't help myself muttering within mouthfuls, *You loathsome fellow! Call me old, damn you! So openly, so brazenly! Old will be thy father, not me, dude! I will see you when your time comes! It'd serve you well!*

'WELL DONE, SENOR!'

The city bus was not overcrowded, but most of the seats were occupied. So, I had to take a seat meant for senior citizens on the front left side of the bus. An elderly lady occupied the window seat alongside me. To add to my peace of mind, two seats meant for the senior citizens and differently-abled persons were still empty. So, there was no immediate danger of losing the seat.

After the first stop, one senior citizen boarded the bus, and to my surprise, instead of taking the empty seat ahead came straight to me mumbling something. I pointed to the seat on the front rows indicating that he might as well occupy it. The elderly gentleman did not budge and muttered something again. I thought I heard the word 'madam' and so surmised that the lady on the window seat was known to him and that he wanted to give her company for the ride. Without much of a protesting mind, I obliged him, and to my luck, one of the seats on the last rows just got empty.

Instinctively, I kept on watching the senior citizen as I sat down on my new address. More surprise was in store.

Instead of sitting down, he again mumbled something to the elderly lady, and the lady got up, too. I was really confused now. *What was he up to?* The elderly woman moved somewhat stiffly toward the seats on the right side of the bus meant for ladies only. I immediately turned my focus to those seats and found that one seat there was empty. As the senior citizen finally sat down satiated on the window seat, everything, suddenly, was revealed to me. I laughed out inside me and I was not able to prevent the amusement infecting my facial contours.

It was a compact plan. While boarding, the senior citizen took in the scenario inside completely and accordingly made his calculated moves. He disposed of me first, which was not at all against the law, and then he eliminated the lady, too, which was also quite logical. His target was plain and simple—to have a comfortable ride occupying the window seat.

Well done, Senor! Keep it up!

THE LONER!

The first head turned. Its eyes were focused on the entrance of the busy roadside restaurant.

The owner of this crucial part of the anatomy had sharp features and other delights too. He was short, rather emaciated, of dark complexion and had a Charlie Chaplin mustache. This latter addition gave the face that belonged to the canine variety a comic look.

It was evening time and the air was thick and suffocating with peak hour traffic.

The first head, as we will call our hero hereafter, was waiting at the bus stop, and the deliberate turning of his head away from the coming buses backward to the restaurant naturally attracted some attention. Its taut positioning and the intent gaze emanating from it appealed to the curious instincts of a lot of fellow commuters. More and more heads started turning in that direction.

The ever-increasing number of heads didn't exactly know what to find or what to expect there, but their collective curiosity was constantly fueled by the undivided attention showered by the first head on the metaphoric sight.

The first head made a sudden move now. He started walking at a brisk pace toward the restaurant. The other heads followed him devotedly with their fixed, expecting stares. They waited impatiently because they wanted to make sure before they decided to make their next moves. Although always drawn on by such curiosity chores daily, they still thought—*why waste time unnecessarily on the prank of some stupid crank?* Being the proud inhabitants of a roaring Indian metropolis, they never ever failed to realize that time was money and if a minute was not to be translated into a few bucks more, they expected to get at least the money's worth for that unproductive time.

After reaching the entrance of the eatery, the first head stopped abruptly and began taking surreptitious peeps into the crowded environs inside. The counter manager was all smiles, and as always, he effortlessly stuck to the eternally welcoming posture.

"Come on in, Sir. Why stop there? A lot of crowds, yes, Sir…natural at this hour! But not to worry—we have tables for you. You can climb up to the AC block for more comfort!"

The first head mumbled something inaudible and continued with his random peeps. The manager persisted.

"Are you looking for your friend, Sir? No issues—please come inside and take a thorough look," the manager was now a little apprehensive. He had been in this business for over two decades and he prided himself in knowing all sorts of customers inside out.

No impact though on this particular one. Again, the mumblings and the peeps continued.

Now, the other heads were sure that something fishy was indeed going on. Some fun was definitely in the offing. Most of the heads started moving toward the restaurant.

The manager was taken aback, failing to classify this particular specimen. Annoyance was slowly robbing him of his placid welcome gestures.

"Please don't mind my saying so, Sir, but you are definitely creating a hindrance right here in this crucial point of entry! We always want to give the very best of service to our customers and we cannot survive otherwise. Please try to understand, Sir! I still welcome you, please come inside and have a seat!"

He paid no attention to the pleading manager.

By now quite a crowd gathered outside the restaurant. There were murmurs, whispers.

"What's happening, pal?"

"How would I know? Let's get nearer still and find out!"

"I knew the fellow was not normal, but I fail to understand what he's up to!"

"Maybe he's plain mad, maybe we're wasting our time!"

Nobody knew why they were all there. However, they were all egged on by their insatiable curiosity—the expected thrill of watching something unique without any cost or without any impending fear of any danger to them arising out of their participation.

Now, a few waiters joined the harassed manager, but even their combined efforts failed to make the first head articulate. The manager eyed the potential customers greedily and wished all of them came inside ordering happily. But alas! Nobody was interested in coming inside the eatery. His annoyance now gave way to glowing embers of anger that stirred within him.

"Hey, what's the fun, huh? You people either come in or disperse! I'm not going to tolerate this kind of infringement on my fundamental right of doing business with freedom, not a minute longer, I warn you!" the manager thundered to the crowd growing in size with every passing second.

There were hostile reactions to the manager's histrionics. To his consternation, there followed a voracious exchange of invectives, and the crowd swelled further. The situation now threatened to go out of control.

Meanwhile, the first head was at total peace with itself and was dexterously carrying on with its sneak preview of the hotel interiors.

Finally, help came in the form of a traffic policeman who shouted his way through in a bid to find out the root cause of the problem. While continuing with his authoritative overtures, he was constantly passing on messages through his walkie-talkie. The manager clutched at this last straw and furnished him with a brief on the issue.

The policeman walked up to the first head and demanded to know what was going on. Failing to give a proper enough justification would mean an instant arrest for creating a law-and-order situation, he warned. The first head now decided to break his silence.

"You see, I'm very lonely and depressed…"

"I don't care how you are; just explain your actions. Quick!"

"…I have no near or dear ones. I live alone in my house, eat alone…sleep alone…passing every minute is a pain for me; I get no appetite…I…"

"Cut it out, bugger! I'm not interested in your background. Stick to the point," now the policeman was getting impatient.

"Please, no abuses! I'm a respectable person. I must stress the point that knowing the background is a must to understand any situation," the hero readied himself to launch into a scholarly discourse. "I told you of my painfully insignificant and mundane existence. But God has a plan for every living being and I was no exception. You see, I fell in love with a beautiful girl who gave a new meaning to my life. Suddenly, I was alive and bursting with energy…"

The policeman was beginning to enjoy now and a grin cracked his dry lips. There were also a few giggles from the crowd. The hero was blissfully oblivious though.

"…I never wanted to lose her; I proposed and she accepted as per God's will. My joy knew no bounds. But I had a fear…am I really going to get so much happiness… the loner that I always was. I was paranoid about losing her…"

"Hold it now, enough of your love story! Do please come to the point, my dear forlorn lovebird," he paused dramatically for effect.

He was rewarded. For a change, there were no giggles.

"As always, I was waiting for a bus this evening, and suddenly I saw her…but I'm not sure…sort of hoping against hope. I desperately want to be proved wrong. I still stand here to confirm…she cannot do this to me… You see, I saw her with a man! I saw both of them entering this very restaurant! If they come out now…and confirm my worst fear…I'll drop dead right here…!"

There was absolute silence for a moment. First, the policeman started it. He bellowed with raucous unleashed laughter. His body shook and tears blocked his eyes. Soon, all in the watching crowd joined in the mayhem merriment.

The manager never wanted to let go of this opportunity. He invited all for a cup of tea and welcomed the now-silent hero to have a thorough search in all corners of the eatery.

However, our hero began to slip away quietly taking advantage of the relieved situation. As he jumped into a running bus, he mumbled to himself, "Abominable nincompoops! Laugh on…you hyenas! How would you know! That this was just good enough fun in my uniquely creative way to have an appetizing supper tonight! Eeeeekh…eeeeeeekh! I'm already feeling hungry, ravenously hungry! Eeeeeeeekh…need food now!"

The restaurant was bubbling with activity. Nobody noticed our hero slipping away.

TWO STRANGERS AT IT

He stared at me; I stared at him back. Our eyes got locked. And he continued to stare at me, and I started feeling a little uneasy and tried to avoid him, roving my eyes here and there, still aware of the fact that he didn't follow my divisionary tactics, his stare unflinching.

We were sitting at a medical clinic on opposite rows, waiting for the doctors' call. This was a multi-specialty clinic, and so the patients were in the common lounge for doctors of various departments. In all probability, my staring stranger was not in the queue for my doctor.

After some time, I stared back at him to check the status; to my dismay, he was still staring at me. My uneasiness gave way to plain resentment now. I had to know why.

I stood up, went over to his side and sat down in the vacant seat next to him. He now looked at me sideways with interest, his face beaming.

"Do you know me?" I asked him, showing my anger.

"In fact, a friend of mine with sharp features and a pointed nose," he began, "resembles you. That's why your face caught my attention... I'm now sure you're not him."

"He is your friend, you say, and you took such a long time to confirm! Your behavior is just not right," I cried.

"Oh, I'm very sorry for that. Please pardon me...you're a good person. I really like you now. Please forget what happened. Tell me, Sir, do you stay nearby?" he sounded truly apologetic.

Mellowing down a bit I replied, "Yes, within a walking distance. What about you?"

"I also stay nearby... Hey! We could just turn out to be neighbors!" he said excitedly.

Then the conversation veered to locations and houses, people and markets, and of course, various local issues and problems.

About half an hour later, the stranger's name was called. He stood up immediately. "Thanks a lot, friend! You know, waiting is a tedious job, you must find a way out to enjoy!" said he with a benign grin and turned toward the doctor's chamber.

Now I could stare only at his back; however, I continued to do so till he vanished inside the cabin. Then, I allowed my lips to crack into a very tight smile, really making an effort at that; I didn't want to invite more stares.

THE HAUNTED PAJAMA!

The boss asked me to come around eight in the evening. Actually, he was not my boss, but one of my good friend's. Once, when I visited my friend in his office, it so happened that the boss came to him on a query, and since I was sitting in his cubicle, he introduced me to the boss—a painter by profession, that is to say. The boss seemed to like me at the very first instance, asking me to come to his chamber for a cup of tea. Lively discussions ensued on creative arts, paintings, the market for artists and so on. I found him to be open-minded and devoid of any air or ego. So, in a way, I liked him too—at the very first instance, that is to say.

Later on, I learned from my friend that the boss, in fact, was a very influential person in society and had tremendous contacts. Considering my not-too-healthy artistic pursuits in recent times, my friend planted an idea in me: *Why not approach him for some references?* He resided in a posh housing society—just a 10-minute walk from my residence. To tell the truth, I needed some connections and references to be able to hold a solo exhibition in the best art gallery in the city and also to take things further in selling my paintings. Naturally then, I clutched at the idea like the proverbial straw.

I visited the boss again in his chamber on the pretext of meeting my friend and after lots of beating-around-the-bush, I finally raised the subject of somewhat seeking a favor from him. To put me at ease, he was very encouraging and told me that a famous cultural figure lived in one of the apartments of his society; he promised to take me to him. He asked me to give him a call before coming, preferably on weekends.

I called him several times in the recent weeks, but always he found an excuse for not being able to entertain me on that day. Although I was a little put-off and frustrated, and although I was not used to seeking or getting favors in my existential struggles, I did not give up.

And finally, he called me home on that evening and promised to take me to the great personality. That was some solace to my sense of self-dignity; I looked forward to the promised meeting.

I pressed the doorbell of his first-floor flat, and I was ushered in by a housemaid. After about ten minutes, he appeared beaming at me and dropped himself on the sofa from a considerable height. He was clad in a home-stitched traditional white pajama with a white vest tucked into it. *Well,* I pondered, *it must be because of the humid heat.* However, I continued with my thoughts, *I do hear a mild whirring sound of ACs in operation inside.* As I looked around, I saw an AC in this sitting room too, but not operating, and the ceiling fan gyrating rather too weakly. *Well,* I continued still, *perhaps the boss avoids expensive ways of treating guests, particularly a non-profitable guest like me.* But in any case,

I was a little disappointed at not finding him dressed and ready.

As he continued smiling at me in a rather worryingly relaxed way, I managed with a gentle query, "Sir, how is everything? …are we going to see him presently?"

"Oh yes, definitely. But there is no hurry as such. He is as nocturnal as me. Ha! Ha!" he bellowed in the same nonchalant way. And he started chattering on a variety of subjects, often not waiting for my response.

After nearly an hour of inanities and my growing impatience, he exclaimed suddenly, "Ah! It's so hot and humid! I really need a bath! Would you mind if I do?"

"Not at all, Sir! Please do!" I replied with the inner-me not at all supporting my response.

Half an hour later, around 9:30 in the evening now, he came back and occupied the sofa in the same way. I was confounded finding him in the same dress—pajama and the vest tucked in. And there had begun another session of banter, my impatience slowly giving way to boiling anger.

Another half-hour elapsed when he exclaimed again, "Oh damn it! I feel very hungry now. We'll surely go to him, but let him also have his supper. Please bear with me…I must!" He withdrew to the dining room inside. For a fleeting moment, I considered storming out but controlled myself hoping for action finally. I continued sitting there, and I was not welcomed even with a glass of water.

Just before eleven in the night, he entered the sitting room again fondly caressing his belly; again, he was clad the same way with the drawstring cord of his pajama dangling out dangerously; again, he crashed into the velvety sofa, overwhelmingly relaxed and again he started one more session of inanities. I could hold it no longer.

About perhaps a ton of ire had been accumulating like phlegm at the middle of my stomach; now it surged up in great fury and it was thanks to my best of efforts that I succeeded in allowing it only to scratch at my throat and stop dead there. The efforts made my countenance rather distorted as I felt my lips curling up, gnawing both jaws, and my eyes almost bulging out. I somehow managed, "Forget it for today…it's got quite late. Good night!" I moved toward the main door without waiting for his response.

"No…no…dear fellow! We can still make it…but if you insist let's do it next time. Please call me…!" the boss's voice trailed off as I stormed out.

Although I was exhaling and inhaling only fury and a temper of the highest order, I couldn't stop myself from laughing out like a mad man on the way back home. I pitied myself, aghast at my apparent helplessness and surrender, and pondered why at all. *Well,* I decided, *one should never do things against one's wishes; one must be on one's own at all times, odd or even…and keeping the exchange of favors at bay.*

And the pajama stopped haunting me.

THE BURPY BLUES

The big boss seemed to be exuding benevolence of the highest order as he took in his company team members seated in front of him in the longish conference room. He often prided himself in knowing every member of his team on a first-name basis, and always listened to their views or problems in a very friendly way. Recently, he initiated an office procedure to improve the overall quality of performance and operations. True to his nature, before implementing this procedure, he wanted to know how everyone felt about it. He wanted free and frank opinions and also meaningful suggestions. So, he called for this particular meeting. Although I was the latest addition to the team, I had already gathered useful bits of information about my new boss.

Again, true as always to his nature, he never wanted to make it a predictable affair with members standing up and speaking in a monotonous serial order—one by one, row-wise. Instead, he decided who would speak at what time. He would announce names at random and s/he would speak accordingly. Therefore, in actual practice, it happened like that one in the very first row would give his/her opinion first and someone in the last or middle rows would be asked to speak next. The benevolent boss also asked his team members to be wary of repetitions—points chosen by earlier speakers must be avoided.

Quite an unusual procedure to discuss an office procedure, I mused sitting in the first row and in direct eye contact with the big boss. I figured rather high in the company hierarchy, the onus thus did not naturally fall upon me to start. It worked rather well. Not knowing exactly when their turn to speak would come, people prepared their points faster, keeping themselves in readiness and making adjustments to avoid repetitions.

Teas and snacks kept on coming in rounds as the discussion went on without any time constraint. *It is important and so time should not be a factor,* the boss announced in the beginning. We happily waited for our turns, sipping tea and munching cakes and savoring sweets.

Suddenly, in the solemn and intent atmosphere, I heard a noise. I immediately deciphered it to be a loud burp and tried to focus quickly on the rather unwelcome source. I traced it to an elderly person who was yet to speak and had only been feasting on the freebies. However, by that time, his action concluded thus depriving me of the intrinsic charms associated with burping or belching.

I always enjoyed such acts, which unfailingly entailed an assortment of facial expressions or contortions. Some would do it full-mouthed and loud, opening out as if to relish every bit of it; others would skew their parted lips either to the left or the right while not at all trying to suppress the noise; someone would kill the noise and release the air smoothly with some movement of the neck, jaw and mouth while most others with etiquette would always hide the action with left or right palm involving the bare minimum of facial contortions.

I thought the big boss would definitely react to it irritably. But nothing of that sort happened, and proceedings went on. In fact, nobody in the assembly displayed any reaction.

And lo! It happened again. Loud and clear! This time somewhere from a row behind me, and I missed the action and the source entirely. I only managed to see a lady sitting opposite looking askance at the source seeming to say, "God! Could it be really you...?"

The big boss displayed no emotion this time too. And the proceedings went on smoothly.

We came to the end of the session, finally. The big boss was satisfied and happy getting mostly what he expected to get. The last round of tea was served. And then it happened.

In the very act of taking a sip from his cup of tea, the big boss had it. He somehow managed to swallow it with an awkward scowl, not succeeding to suppress the noise, however. It was again a loud act of belching.

Very compassionate, I concluded with satisfaction and great amusement.

A PUNCH IN THE LURCH

Shyam arrived unannounced, as usual. Ram got really annoyed that evening as he had an important task to accomplish, his son being away on an excursion. *This fellow is incorrigible! We meet five days a week in the office and yet he lands up almost every evening!* Ram thought ruefully. His problem was accentuated because his wife and children loved passing time with Shyam.

Ram welcomed him, as always, and Shyam sank lazily in the comfortable cushioned chair. He started talking immediately; nothing of importance, as always. However, that evening, Ram was determined not to entertain his visitor for long. Before his wife could emerge, he went inside, and said, "Give him all the pastries, sweetmeats and salted delicacies with the tea, so that he loses his appetite for supper." His wife smiled with a wink and agreed.

Snacks came, tea came; but the visitor seemed to be in no hurry to leave. Ram was fidgeting, getting impatient as the clock ticked on. He seemed to hear a moaning sound, which made him restless. In his family tradition, Ram never learned to be hostile to a guest, always entertaining them, often missing or delaying important engagements. Besides,

Shyam was a colleague and a good friend working in the same production house.

As the clock struck eight, Ram could withstand no more. The pitiful moaning had been more frequent in the last hour. He stood up.

"I'd rather take out my doggie for his customary evening stroll," he announced summarily.

Shyam looked up at him, a bit surprised, and said gravely, "If I were you, I'd rather sit down for some time."

"What for?" Ram almost cried.

"Sit down first, dear friend. I have something important to tell you," he waited for Ram to sit down. "Three days back, you punched that guy, Ravi, you know… in office!"

Yes, Ram knew it very well. He had broken his nose, and he had been bunking office since then. Ravi was an extremely lazy yet cunning and slippery fellow; he always thrived on trying to steal credit for others' work and knew how to oil his bosses.

That day there was a crucial program meeting with the regional boss, and all new ideas were to be discussed. Ram called for an initial meeting with his colleagues presenting a few of his own ideas for concurrence before formally presenting these to the boss.

Everything went wrong in the crucial meet for Ram, however. Immediately after the boss's motivational speech, Ravi instantly started narrating all the ideas presented by Ram earlier as his own, proudly, and got tremendous appreciation from the boss. Ram, thunderstruck, could only manage, "Yes, Sir, we discussed these ideas already. Actually…" he broke off knowing very well that anything he uttered in favor of himself would only present him as petty and envious.

Therefore, after the meeting, he simply went up to Ravi's desk, punched him furiously on his nose and stomped out of the office.

"...he threatened you that he would lodge a police complaint, no?" Shyam continued. "But first he went to the hospital, and then home to consult his wife. At the sight of his bandaged nose, his wife went into hysterics. She was uncontrollably happy that someone had done what she could never ever have accomplished herself. She felt like an avenging angel, as it were. But then, the surprise of surprises! She started taking very good care of him, so much so that their eternally strained married life became healthy and joyous. And my friend, I'm carrying Ravi's compliments for you this evening. He is so grateful for your resounding punch; a game-changer, I say!"

Ram couldn't react at all for some time, sitting as if transfixed. Then he started laughing, hollering.

"Enjoy your moment with your wife, pal!" Shyam put in happily. "Let me take out your doggie. The poor loyal fellow does not want to dirty his master's house, ever!" he turned around again and said to Ram, "In the meantime, the boss came to know fully what's what! So, you can join office tomorrow without fear!"

Still laughing, Ram cried out, "No problem, buddy. Thanks. Come back and have supper with us!"

THE PECULIAR MYSTERY OF A PARCEL

The last few days had been very irritating for him. There had been a lot of festival-season work pressure, every day, not even sparing the weekends or the holidays. He had been at it continuously from morning to late night daily, and on top of it, one more vexing issue had cropped up haunting him for the last three days with continuous calls and reminders from his head office. He had no clue whatsoever about this issue yet.

In the office hierarchy, Chandan had been the third-in-command. But in actuality, he alone had had to run the office for nearly a month, simply because the top boss of this very important branch of the national television channel had been on sick leave for over a month now, and the second-in-command, as was usual with him, had been taking it too easy, running his family business from the office facilities. The second-in-command's ecstasy knew no bounds as he had been allowed to operate from the chamber of the top boss, and he contentedly assumed the airs of the supreme boss, de facto though. So, Chandan had to run to that chamber for the final decisions on every matter, and every time he did so, he was flustered by the not-a-bother ease of the second-in-command. Chandan had to consult him, too, on that vexing issue, and what he earned in the bargain was an expression of great and benign amusement.

Three days back, Chandan had received a call from the headquarters to the effect that a high-priority parcel was couriered already and an immediate acknowledgment was required: the parcel contained new logos of the company to be used in all coverage or interview programs this festival season. Chandan replied that the parcel was not received till then and that he would immediately intimate on receipt.

The next day, too, the parcel did not arrive, and the calls became more frequent and demanding. Chandan asked for the courier details, and after receiving them, he instantly called up the courier company with the consignment number. To his surprise, he was informed that the parcel was delivered yesterday and was received at the office. The company could not specify the name of the person who received it.

Irritated and angered beyond measure now, Chandan created an uproar in the office interrogating everyone for the package, from the personal assistant of the top boss to all staff and executives and the peons/messengers/security personnel. To his frustration, nobody admitted having received or seen the said parcel. Chandan said sorry to the head office that for some unknown reasons the parcel was still not delivered to his office, reluctant to admit that it was received and then went missing. Things were getting tricky. The head office had already sent notes asking for action-taken reports on the use of the new logos.

Chandan sat dejected and gloomy at his chamber on the third day today. He looked at the heaps of files on his desk in disdain, not having the will to go through those. His mind was in turmoil about the missing parcel. *How could a parcel, obviously of a noticeable size since it supposedly contained at least twenty logos with the handles, just vanish into thin air? Besides, nobody could hope to gain anything by stealing it because these would be of no use for others outside his company,* he reasoned further.

He went to the personal assistant's room, and sat with the guy for quite some time, trying to convince him of the importance, urging him to find it at any cost. He could no longer digest the scene—with the assistant constantly shaking his head and occasionally tapping on his computer keyboard—and stormed back to his chambers.

During the lunch hour, as Chandan was trying to thrust in the bits of the homemade *rotis* through his dry and tense throat, the personal assistant burst into his room, carrying a package.

"Oh, Sir! I found it at last…!"

"Thank God! But where and how did you manage to find it?" I said with immense relief, now the grubby bits going down smoothly.

"Under the table of the boss!"

"What? What do you mean?"

"Yes, Sir! It was just lying there…!" the assistant put the parcel on his table and went out, *a bit too hurriedly perhaps,* Chandan thought.

Questions arose in his mind: *How? The de facto boss had been sitting there all the time! How could it be placed under the table without his notice or attention? What prompted the assistant to go finding it in that particular place?* And all that.

Then it struck him. During the festival season, most of the clients and stakeholders of the channel sent across lots of packaged gifts for the top boss who was rather too fond of receiving those. In his absence, the gifts had accumulated and overflowed the space under his desk. On so many occasions Chandan noticed it and often cracked his lips wryly at the sight of the second-in-command trying to stretch and relax his legs through the tiny space under the table left by the mushrooming gift parcels.

Now he could see it more clearly. Somebody did receive the parcel, thought it was just another gift and stacked it under the table, perhaps when the second-in-command was not there or perhaps the latter also thought it was a gift. His doubt was focused now on the personal assistant who must have done that, and not admitting the same for the fear of being held liable for disciplinary action for dereliction of duty. However, Chandan decided to not pursue the issue with the assistant any further. The parcel was found and was safe, which was the most important thing.

Chandan got into action right away: calling the local representatives to come personally and collect the new logos; asking the dispatch clerk to courier the logos to the outstation representatives immediately.

By evening, Chandan sat relaxed sipping his steaming cup of tea. He could not help smiling now and then, thinking over the whole episode of the mysterious parcel. *How nobody, including himself, could ever think of checking the piles of the parcels under the table of the top boss for once?* He wondered. Perhaps it was the 'under the table' stigma that shooed off all beholders instantly. Chandan laughed out.

THE CHEERLESS CHAUFFEUR

I heard a car coming to a stop outside, and the familiar sound of banging a door shut. Waves of the mild morning breeze wafted into the dining room of the guest house, momentarily parting the door curtains, just enough for me to behold out of the corners of my eyes, a tall and athletic figure striding toward us. I continued to concentrate fully on my plateful of bread and scrambled eggs as the man came in. *Well, being his boss, both in terms of rank and age, I should never look up to his arrival or keep looking at him with expectations and queries,* I reasoned.

The man accosted, "Good morning, Sir," from the doorway and advanced toward our table in the spacious dining room. Closer now, he greeted my wife warmly. I asked him to occupy a seat and invited him to have breakfast with us. He settled for a cup of tea as he said he had had a full meal before leaving home. As we ate, he gave me a brief of the day's schedule ahead, and we also discussed a few other office matters.

A kind of curiosity had been gnawing at my mind all the time: *What kind of car has he arranged for the trip, which includes several destinations on business-cum-pleasure discretion and is likely to take up the full day!* I had been used to...or rather used to watching chauffeur-driven limousines waiting to take in very important people, everywhere on the TV or computer or mobile screens, and of course, I had myself arranged similar cars for our global big bosses on a few occasions. Well, in my case, I didn't realistically expect that kind of treatment. Yes, I was the boss of the regional headquarters with several branch offices under my command, but that type of bosses abounded in our country, and the chauffeur-driven luxury cars were never economical or affordable options. Besides, this city where I came on an inspection tour was quite small, perhaps not at all infested with wonderful cars, and was only known for a few famous tourist sites scattered around it. Anyway, I decided to call him a chauffeur, not a mere driver, whatever be the type of car arranged.

We finished our breakfast and came out. Since we had come down prepared for the journey, there was no need of going back to our room. The executive, Ranjit by name, led the way, and finally, I had the *darshan* of the vehicle meant for me.

It was an Innova! No problems! The 'usual car' being replaced wisely by an 'SUV' soothed my ego or whatever airs I was supposedly entertaining within or transmitting. I looked forward to enjoying the treatment normally meted out to superior executives, like, you know, bowing and throwing the doors open for the guests to take the seats and closing the doors on them ever so softly, and then going around the car for the other seats in the front side. But where the heck is the 'chauffeur'? I looked around fervently, not able to find anyone of that order, preferably uniformed and approaching.

Actually, nothing of that sort of 'treatment' happened. I found the 'chauffeur' sitting inside the vehicle and rather curiously, was slumped over the wheel in his driving seat. He did not even bother to look up at me as we approached. Ranjit stood aside and waited as I opened the door for my wife to board, then I seated myself and shut the door. Ranjit then occupied the front passenger seat. The car started veering slowly toward the exit gate, and we were on our way.

Traffic was not much that day being a Sunday. The vehicle moved at a good speed, mostly uninterrupted. I looked out of my side window to catch glimpses of life in the place that we visited for the first time. Suddenly, the car jerked violently.

I looked out of the windscreen instinctively. Why, there was no obstruction or traffic anywhere, no cars following or overtaking and none closely ahead! I watched the chauffeur…no, the driver, for a clue, found nothing unusual except for the fact that he seemed to be slumped farther down his seat. As I wondered about how the driver, short and stocky, managed to have a vision through the windscreen, it happened again: this time it was a distinct swerve toward the divider, and the driver had to wheel the vehicle quickly to his left and adjust the movement. Slightly concerned now, I decided to observe him closely. And my concern turned to fright.

The driver was taking a nap at the wheel as his head dipped suddenly, the first time under my taut observation, and then again…and again! I was now seriously concerned about the safety of us all. I looked at Ranjit, but he was immersed in his smartphone. My mind raced as to what could be done calmly and discreetly. I didn't want to raise an alarm, because shouting from a stranger would've disturbed the driver further, and most importantly, it would greatly agitate my wife, which I never desired. I found a plan.

I sent a text message to Ranjit asking him to watch the driver and to alert him in his mother tongue, and not to discuss the matter publicly yet. Luckily, Ranjit read the message immediately and began watching the driver. The car did the jerks again twice, and Ranjit got the point now. He began to talk to the driver in soft tones, and the slumped driver seemed to have nodded. However, I saw him dipping his head again.

No, the danger is too great for a discreet silence now, I thought. And I made it public, loud and clear. As I expected, my wife got unduly alarmed. To stamp my authority, I ordered the car to stop immediately in front of a tea-shop, and that the driver must take a hot cup of strong tea.

The vehicle came to a stop accordingly at the first tea-joint we could find on the highway. We got down and I ordered the driver to accompany us. We sat down on the bamboo bench and ordered tea for all of us. The driver mumbled something to Ranjit.

"Sir, he won't take tea!" Ranjit ventured.

"No! He must!" I announced, irritably.

"But, Sir, he says he never drinks tea!"

"Is coffee available or red tea here?"

"No, Sir! He doesn't take any stimulant like that!"

"Damn it!" I muttered in anger, searching for an alternative. The driver was standing listlessly by our side. Then, to my horror, his head dipped. *My God! He's napping even while standing,* I couldn't believe it. In my desperation, I found the alternative.

"Ranjit, give him a strong *paan* then! He cannot just refuse it! He's sleeping even when standing!"

This time Ranjit did not consult him, and bought a *paan* (a betel nut-betel leaf-lime concoction with other optional sweet ingredients and even grades of tobacco) from the nearby shop and ordered him to swallow and chew it. The driver had to do accordingly. I was satisfied now, somewhat.

The journey resumed. I was happier now seeing the driver sitting a little erect in his seat, still chewing. For a moment, I felt sorry to have forced him into it but, I justified, our safety was the prime concern. I wondered what could be the reason for his present pitiable state of affairs, particularly for a professional chauffeur...no, driver. *Perhaps,* my mind raced, *he had a trip yesterday running into late-night hours or he enjoyed a binge party or a wedding party drinking freely and overeating, and he could not have enough sleep as this trip must have come up for him unexpectedly. Yes, it's acute acidity,* I decided.

Then I heard a peculiar sound from the driver's seat, a kind of a throaty expression, which was normal for any human being. I heard it again, and again. A sharp, feminine but coarse sound! As it kept on coming at a disciplined frequency, I finally could diagnose it. Yes, it was a hiccup of an acute nature. I felt sorry again but justified it again as the price for our safety.

The hiccups that never left him alone for the next several hours kept him fully awake. He sat more and more erect as its intensity increased. It ensured our safety for the rest of the day. I reclined now against the luxuriously comfortable back-seat with a smile, fully relaxed. Seeing me smile, my wife presented me with a slightly scornful look. I waved it off easily as if mouthing it to her, "It's primarily your safety issue, darling!"

THE RAIN DRENCH!

One of my best friends and I were posted in our common hometown for some time in the long past. It had been a rollicking reunion for us, parted since the college days when my friend went abroad for higher studies and joined a job in a metro city while I completed my higher studies within the country and then joined a transferrable job in my hometown. This effectively meant that we reunited after about six years. There followed regular meetings, parties, family get-togethers and mutual personal visits between our two homes.

I greatly enjoyed going to his home and spending time with his family. Cultured-educated-liberal is what perfectly described the members of his family: his mother actively took part in our talks or discussions, and at the same time, never failed to treat us to sumptuous dishes; his two sisters were very frank, talkative and free of inhibitions; the elder sister doing a part-time job and engaged, and the younger sister was studying in the university; only his father, a government servant, was somewhat taciturn, but never disturbed our sessions.

The good times continued for about a year when my friend got a new job in a neighboring country and left within a fortnight to join what he considered to be a pretty good offer. I missed his family more than I missed him, really. My trips to his home stopped because without the common link, I found it odd to visit them. Or they too might have found it rather odd had I continued my visits. *What could possibly be my goal of visiting them without the best of friends there?* Well, it could be argued that in all that time we passed together I found them very companionable and warm. However, with two grown-up good-looking smart girls there, anybody could've discovered ulterior designs, considering the conservative society we lived in those days. The concept of 'brotherly love' or even platonic love was alien then. So, in a way, it was mutually agreed upon, never verbally though, that the visits should stop.

Within the next year, I too got transferred to a far-off metro city, and everything about the family remained a sweet memory only. On the other hand, my family started getting all the focus as I had to part with them for the second time. The sweet-home syndrome gained predominance.

I was in my hometown about three years later on a long holiday visit as my marriage was being considered actively. Only I was not able to make up my mind. I argued with my parents that I was not yet financially established in the metro, and so one more year would do me good. They argued back that at least the girl could be finalized and the marriage would take place as I desired. I had to agree to that.

During that visit, one incident happened that really shook me up. It left me in a helpless state of mind, not able to communicate effectively, to clarify things perhaps. Those days there were no cell phones or instant messaging facilities or social media. The only 'communication' thing that existed was the black formidable-looking instrument that could not even be called a landline those days; it was just a 'phone', which, in reality, was limited to a few lucky souls like the high-ranking government officials or the very affluent ones. One existed in my home, of course. But it was used mostly for official purposes, and we didn't have a list like today of family and friends' numbers and anyway, most of them didn't have the black box. Thus, I had to pass my days, fretting and fuming.

That fateful day, I had to go out in the morning for an important work at the bank. It was a cloudy day, but as the preceding days had been dull like this without rain, I decided against taking the umbrella with me.

It was around noontime when I finished my work and came out. A situation like 'darkness at noon' greeted me as black clouds covered the entire sky, and rain was imminent. It was a five-minute walk to the bus stop. I took the decision to take the risk without spending time regretting the lack of an umbrella and started walking briskly.

As I neared my destination, light raindrops started falling. I began a half-run when I heard someone calling me from the other side of the road. It was a sweet lively voice. Without stopping, I looked toward the source and had to stop on my tracks.

The younger sister of the best of my friends was standing there with an open umbrella, perhaps heading homewards. She kept looking at me with an expression of joy and surprise. My heart almost exploded with ecstasy. I raced toward her negotiating expertly with the coming and going vehicles. I was successful in crossing the road in quick time, and I stood face to face with her.

A fervent exchange of pleasantries and tidings followed naturally; it was a reunion after three years. As luck would have it, the raindrops became heavier and thicker now. I had no intention of letting her go so soon, and so as I talked excitedly, I started inching toward her in the hope of getting a shelter under her umbrella.

To my horror, she started moving backward as I inched forward. *She was not allowing me to come under her umbrella even as it was apparent that I was getting thoroughly drenched by now.*

Then perhaps, she took pity on me and announced a hasty goodbye. I stood there transfixed for some time, but as the rain-water started dripping into my insides I had to make an equally hasty retreat to the shelter shed of the bus stop.

My brotherly love thwarted, so rudely…so inhumanely…! my heart moaned. I just couldn't accept that. *Why? Was something wrong with me? Did my body language speak something entirely different to her, always? Was my 'brotherly love' a sham?*

The flood of questions created in my innards a web as thick as the heavy rains created outside at the moment. Then, my mind started reasoning as to why she should have behaved like that from her point of view. Perhaps, she had been trying to avoid known faces confronting her with a man under the same umbrella on the streets during a time of heavy showers or perhaps she thought the rains were going to be heavier and wanted me better protected in the bus stop or perhaps she was truly in a hurry, rains or no rains.

Then I felt angry. I decided to tell my mother to hasten up the bride-finding and hold the wedding in the coming months, if possible. Hark! *Why do I have this seemingly unrelated thought?* I pondered. *Or was it related all the time?* I didn't know and I had no intention of pursuing this thread any further. The sight of an invitingly half-empty bus approaching the stop freed me of all my problems, instantly. For the time being, that is to say.

THE MUNCHING WAYS OF
A MISER

He was employed with a good monthly salary, but he always wanted to save every paisa of it, never withdrawing anything from the bank. By hook or by crook! Of course, at times he failed, and on those occasions, he went for the cheapest possible options or preferred to forego the comforts or eating altogether.

He never wanted to pay a monthly rent on accommodation because he felt it was a dead draw from his bank accounts with no productive benefits. He only went in the night to sleep there. So, why pay money for that mundane detail? He was a perfect manager for such tasks.

Initially, in his official existence, he forced himself on a friend and began staying with him in the city of his employment. He managed for a reasonable period constantly telling his friend that it was only a temporary arrangement. However, that place was quite at a distance from his office, and he had to incur daily expenses on public transport. He heartily hated that and was desperate for a solution.

He found one soon. Discovering another friend with a house very near to his office, he again forced himself with the same modus operandi. He was elated at being able to save all his salary plus taking healthy daily walks to his office. As far as the 'food for living at no cost' or 'munch management' was concerned, he concentrated on the events or programs or seminars or conferences or parties where at least one of the three meals was guaranteed. Those events mostly took care of his free breakfasts and lunches. He thoroughly relished those meals that were 'free unlimited downloads' for him! As for the suppers, he participated joyfully whenever his friend decided to cook at home. On occasions when dinners could not be ensured, he preferred to remain hungry and healthy for the next free meal the next day.

He would take only mineral water on robust health grounds. Office provided that facility free of cost with the water jars coming in daily. He collected free bottles, filled those with the office water and took those to his house. He considered the tap water there unsafe for drinking.

On weekends, he visited his native town and feasted on the food fiesta offered by his doting mother who was amicably able thanks to her husband's good pension. Our miser showed implacable dexterity in avoiding the expenses of his weekly bus trips to his native place too by managing a government pass, forcing the office clerks to oblige him.

He never entertained any thought of getting married after arguing it out conclusively for himself, *I'll never marry an unemployed girl…obviously because her daily food requirement will be a dead burden on me! Even if I marry an employed woman, I'll naturally become her finance manager…*

and her money will be my money! But, this too is bound to take
a turn for the worse because of our mutual food requirements…
involving buying of foods I never prefer!

Once, he was really caught in an ominous wedlock
situation due to the insistence of his parents. True to his
frugal abilities, he managed to wriggle out, convincing his
parents that the marriage could result in him being taken
away from them for good by the wife.

On office days, when he failed to manage 'free meal'
events, he existed on biscuit bites. At times, he bought the
cheapest biscuit packets available or collected those from
safe sources and stockpiled them in his room for future
use. On some occasions, he used to sit continuously in
the room of his boss purportedly for selfless advice and
companionship. The boss invariably ordered lunch at the
appointed hours, and because our miser continued to sit,
he was offered food as a rendered-compulsory gesture of
hospitality. He ravenously coveted office tours, because all
his needs were taken care of free for days. On rare occasions,
when he failed miserably to arrange free food or even
biscuits, he magnanimously decided to starve during the
day. We mentioned this fact earlier concerning the nights.

One night, his friend went to dine out without
informing him. As he entered the house, he had to face this
extremely unpleasant fact. He cursed himself for not having
the foresight of keeping some biscuits at the house too. We
forgot to mention one important fact—our miser never
took tea. If this decision was habitual or made in light of
the consideration of the concomitant costs was not known.
Anyway, this 'habit' or 'decision' saved him loads of money
in terms of having teas himself and/or offering those to

guests. Then he brightened up. He managed an invitation for a forenoon seminar the next day where at least breakfast would be provided.

Coming to the office, he immediately rushed to the venue only to find that the fixture was canceled at the last minute due to unavoidable reasons. He asked his assistant for a cheap restaurant nearby. On being told that there was no such restaurant in the immediate vicinity, he came back to the office dejected, depressed and ravenously hungry. He dashed to his boss's room for humanitarian considerations only to find it empty. He slumped in his room chair and gulped down a few biscuits with some free water.

His food situation worsened in the evening as he found his friend out on a date with a girlfriend. Later, he somehow got hold of the soft copy of an invitation for an important event the next day, starting before the lunch hour. He decided to starve that night too in the hope of the 'free unlimited download' the next day. His mind was in turmoil for some other rickety reasons. He could not contact his boss for the formal assignment to attend the next day's event. *Maybe some other person will get the assignment or have already got*, he pondered anxiously. He had to ensure it come what may. His starving body called for desperate measures.

He rushed to his office very early in the morning, waited eagerly for his boss to arrive. The moment the boss entered, he barged into the chamber almost clamoring for assignment mercy. Eliciting a formal nod, he preferred not to meet or inform any other executives in the office for possible delay or confusion and literally ran to the venue.

Whether our miser finally got his free meal and accomplished the 'free unlimited download' at the conclusion of the event was not immediately known.

A BLUFF OF THE HAZARDOUS KIND

The heavy rains pounded on the glass window panes, making them shudder and tremble under the relentless impact. Shades of the green could be seen through the blurred panes as a strong accompanying wind swept the tree branches across. It was just past eleven in the morning, but the black enveloping clouds and the intense showers made it almost dark with some of the street lights and lights inside many of the flats coming to life again. The din and the gloom reigned supreme.

Gautam continued to sit glumly on a wooden chair in the hall of his one-bedroom flat. Although the darkness had infiltrated the room completely, he did not bother to switch on the lights, as if the gloom inside him were at total peace with the gloom outside. His mind was in turmoil, and he had no clue what to do next.

The heavy rainstorm started just half an hour after his wife left home with their seven-year-old son, on a visit of immense importance. The landlady served them with a vacation notice as per which they'd have to vacate their rented flat within a month. His little family was shattered by that bolt from the blue. At that particular time, they could never think of vacating or moving to a new house even in the wildest of their dreams. Gautam was still recovering from the lockdown blues during which he was put on without-pay status from the third month of the lockdown. For the last two months, after things were gradually unlocked, he had been doing overtime for the shoe production company to somehow make up the huge salary losses.

The landlady was generous too, on many previous occasions. She waived half of the monthly house-rent from the month he went without pay, on his wife's request. Gautam avoided thinking about why the landlady turned so cruel all of a sudden. Instead, he wanted to repose full faith in his wife's persuading ability, her genuine pleas. And that was the problem.

The landlady lived a few miles away from that building of rented flats. His wife was to travel by the city bus. Now, he was not at all sure if she had boarded the bus or reached the landlady's residence before the deluge started. Her mobile was also coming switched off. Gautam's anxiety grew as the minutes ticked by and a sense of helplessness nearly overpowered him, unable to contact her, ignorant about their safety and tortured by the impending crisis.

The doorbell rang suddenly, its sound muffled by the pounding outside. Hoping against hope, Gautam rushed to open the door. He nearly cursed aloud after beholding the visitor.

The newspaper agent was standing there with an odd grin and a crumpled piece of paper in his hands that was probably the monthly bill, his raincoat dripping water from all sides. He deposited his umbrella against the wall at the corner of the passage, and a rivulet already formed streaming from the umbrella down the staircase. *Oh my God! What a time to come collect money! Has this fellow gone raving mad?* Gautam thought in apparent disapproval and disappointment. However, he did not utter anything to that effect, and simply took the bill and paid him off, in a heavily sound-tracked silence.

Gautam sat hunched for two more hours, not even yielding to the urge of a hot cup of tea due at this hour. He also stopped dialing his wife's mobile, the futility of the exercise being more painfully infuriating. In the meantime, the rains were reduced to a drizzle and the light improved considerably. When the doorbell rang again then, he was almost sure that it must be them.

He opened the door immediately. His wife entered and went straight past him into the kitchen getting busy instantly and handling the utensils rather roughly. His little son went straight for the TV remote and switched the set on.

Gautam chased his wife into the kitchen.

"Dear me! What happened?" he managed to mouth. She remained gruff and silent, preparing for a late lunch. He repeated his query several times, getting all the more anxious. Finally, she broke her sullen silence.

"Why! You'd know better! It's all of your doing!"

"God! What have I done?"

"Don't pretend to be the lovable innocent neighborhood boy! You did it without my knowledge, and didn't even bother to tell me afterward! Why the hell you had to issue a threat to that generous lady?"

He remembered the incident perfectly.

CRSO

For more than a year, quite a few persisting problems in their rented flat haunted them. The water taps were not working properly, the kitchen sink was leaking, there was expanding seepage in the bedroom ceiling infecting the electric switchboard and leading to short circuit several times, and there were newer cracks in the walls of all the rooms. They had called the landlady and told her about the issues several times but to no avail. Then, the lockdown delayed it beyond tolerance level. And then, when repair professionals were slowly being allowed inside the flats, they reminded her again and again, but again no action.

The glaringly pending issues made them irritable, and they often had bitter quarrels. At times, Gautam returned from work and coming face to face with the issues immediately sat fuming and fretting, starting a loud monologue of invective against the usual indifference of all landlords or landladies. Often, his wife added fuel to his fire.

"Why sit angry like this in your own kingdom! Do you have the courage to go to her personally, tell her convincingly and entreat her for solutions? Don't waste your energy in futile outbursts, learn to be assertive!"

One day it hit him really hard, and he announced instantly he would go to her the next day itself.

And he went as announced. The landlady welcomed him cordially offering him a warm cup of team. However, he insisted on coming to the point straightaway.

"Madam! We're really fed up with the problems in our flat. We told you and reminded you a hundred times! My wife and I are really stressed…!"

"Oh, I'm really very sorry! Okay done. I'll send for the plumber and others as soon as possible!"

"How soon, Madam? Can you please specify a date?"

The landlady looked a bit irritated now. "It's not possible to decide instantly on such matters, you know. I'll do it sooner than later, rest assured."

Gautam's ego flared up at that point. He said, blurting out, "The usual response again! It's back to square one now! Sorry, madam, we can't wait any longer! Make it now else we'll vacate the house within the month!"

The landlady was angry at this direct assault. She said in a decisive voice, "No problems. Please vacate the house within one month, and I'm sure you'll definitely get a much better house and a much better landlady!" she rose, apparently dismissing him.

Gautam sat there for some time, horror-struck. Then he managed to mumble out, "No, madam! Please understand, it's only out of accumulated frustration…!"

"You see, I too have my share of frustration and many other problems to attend to. However, I don't ever put the burden of my frustration on others! Please leave! It's final! Vacate my flat within thirty days! Nothing more or nothing less!"

ᘉᘏᘉᘏ

"You know, how frustrated and angry we were for more than a year, and you only teased my ego asking me to be assertive! I didn't tell you because it'd have caused more problems, destroyed our peace of mind! Yes, I admit, I was scared of telling you this fact!" Gautam tried to assuage his wife's feelings.

"Wow! What a climbdown of ego! Well, I did tell you to be assertive in the right sense of the word, but definitely not to issue threats, bluffs and what not…!"

"Sorry…sorry…dear! What's past is past! Now let us face the future and the challenges ahead! Tell me, when do we have to vacate? I'll manage somehow. Don't worry. And I mean it this time!"

His wife kept silent for two long minutes, filling the pressure cooker with the containers and putting it on the burner. For a moment, Gautam thought he saw a slight cracking of her lips. He was not sure if it were a smile or a jeer. He stood there as if transfixed, waiting for her to say something. Finally, she broke her silence, "Well, you must acknowledge my efficiency… in all fields of activities, not just housekeeping and cooking! You see, she always had a soft corner for me, respect for my personality and manners. Yes, I convinced her about us, not saying too much about our supposed helplessness either. We need not vacate…and the plumber will come this weekend. The others…one by one, later."

Gautam jumped in ecstasy grabbing her from behind in a tight embrace. She shook him off but smiling now. Their son announced from the hall that he was very hungry.

THE SPIT-FIRE

Even the closed bedroom door could not shield the shrill of the doorbell. I woke up and switched on my mobile to check the time. It was very early. We had been new to the place and the visits of the usual newspaper vendor or the milkman or the maid or the laundry guy had not yet been formalized. *Who could it be?* I got up and trudged lazily to the door. I felt happy that my wife was still sleeping peacefully. I closed the bedroom door behind me, and as I did so, the repeated shrill of the doorbell caught me squarely. That someone outside had to be an impatient customer.

I opened the main door and was surprised to find our landlord right in front. His short and thin figure was upright; his longish face with a hairline mustache showed unmistakable signs of agitation, and his eyes, still puffy from sleep, were blazing.

"Good morning!" I began customarily.

He ignored it completely, "This has never ever happened in my house! How is this possible?"

"What happened…?"

"Just cannot imagine! Preposterous…crazy…!" He paused for effect shaking his head in all possible directions.

"Hello, mister, would you please tell me whatever may have happened and which concerns us!" I could not hide my irritation at this unexpected disturbance at the start of the day.

"Okay, see for yourself! Please follow me…"

I did so, moving with him to the concrete passage running along the front side of the building. Out through the grilled entrance he stopped at the center of the passage, looked down at the ground on both sides angrily. He motioned me to do the same.

Then only I realized the cause of his agitation. There were two big sprawling red spots on both sides of the concrete floor just behind the main gate. Instantly I identified these as *paan* spit—a rush of reddish saliva caused by chewing a heady mix of betel nut, betel leaf, lime and with or without tobacco. *But why was he telling me all this? How on earth could I be held responsible?*

"Oh! Someone has dirtied your compound with *paan* spit. Such sort of people always does it on the corridors, on the lifts…"

He cut me short, "As I told you, this has never happened at my house in my memory! You came in a few days back, and since then a lot of people visited this house for the odd jobs and re-dos as you ordered. You see…!"

Yes, I saw it clearly now. As he claimed this had never happened earlier and so it had to be one of those plumbers, electricians and other vendors we called in. He continued, "Please ask them, quiz them…who must have done this obnoxious thing! Don't spare them! I'm certain that one of your people did this!" And now, I found this term of 'your people' really obnoxious! Temper was slowly rising within me, which I controlled…rather I had to because we were new and this should never turn into a confrontation. As I was searching for the ideal thing to say, the caretaker joined us with a bucket of water and a broom, to my escape. He looked up ruefully at me, "Finally, I have to do the cleaning up!" The landlord decided to stay on to supervise.

My wife was up and about when I entered and narrated the episode. She had a hearty laugh and welcomed the landlord's zeal for cleanliness. I agreed. It had been a national campaign to make your surroundings spick and span. However, I couldn't agree with the accusing tone in the landlord's otherwise righteous agitation.

Over the next few days, we did ask our normal visitors with the expectation that nobody would confess doing it even if s/he did. We also warned newcomers never to do this type of misdeed. During this period, we also noticed a significant decline in our visitors. Quite a few of them, in fact, didn't turn up at all for some much-needed touch-ups in the jobs they had done earlier. I was getting concerned knowing well that the family of the landlord must have been on the job too. One day, our temporary maid confirmed my fears. She confided to my wife that she was quizzed by the landlord's wife if she or any of us two had the chewing habit. I decided to have a talk with the landlord.

The agitation was no longer in him that day and I was happy to see that. I came to the point straightaway.

"Look, mister. It's a very good thing that you are so concerned about cleanliness and we wholeheartedly support this. But we're pained that you're pointing the finger at us. Even if any of us has this habit, why should you be suspicious about us? We're responsible citizens and we'll never litter our own surroundings. You see, the lane outside your gate is a public place and any of the passers-by could be doing this, out of habit or for mischief. And, it is not possible for you or us to monitor them throughout the day. So please don't scare off our visitors. Few of the jobs are still half-done. You see, harassment should never be a part of any good thing you must be doing. Hope you understand!"

If he understood, he didn't show any sign to that effect. He only nodded his head several times uttering some monosyllables. I let it rest at that. If you rented a place, then the landlord was your true boss, and as the saying goes, the boss is always right. And, it was hardly the time to look for a new house.

MILORD...O' LANDLORD

The local landlord was known for his fastidiousness. Although some would like to term it eccentricity. Whatever it be he had been extremely choosy in finalizing his clients. He had several small flats for rent in his building, and he always preferred non-local hassle-free renters in his own unique way.

His terms and conditions were very clear, if not transparent. Visitors/guests staying overnight were a strict no-no; water with a predetermined liter-limit given only once, mostly in the dead of the night; main gates would be locked at 10 p.m. every night and anyone coming late must inform in advance; CCTV cameras on the campus observing irregular activities, and playing or singing of loud music not at all preferred. By profession, he and his wife were teachers, and maybe he took his profession too seriously. He had three young children—two boys and one daughter.

One of his flats was going to be vacated soon and the word spread easily by mouth in the small city. Normally, he engaged a broker who would fix up clients and on approval would charge a fee separately.

Hearing from a friend, one young man approached the landlord directly. The landlord preferred to keep him outside the house while having the initial talk or interview.

"Hey, you need a house?"

"Yes sir, a friend told me one flat will be vacated in two days."

"Right! What do you do?"

"Sir, I'm a businessman in the supply chain contracts."

"How long have you been here? Are you a local?"

"No, I'm not a local and have been here only two years on business."

"Good!" he paused, seemingly assured, and to the client's surprise. "How many in your family?" he resumed his quiz.

"Only myself and my wife, Sir."

"No issues, no?" he asked eagerly.

"No… not so far. Hopefully, we'll have in the near future!"

The landlord suddenly stiffened. "Sorry, in that case, I cannot allow you here!"

Taken aback, the client was as astonished as he was disappointed. "But why, Sir?"

"Well, you see! You'll have a baby and he or she will grow up fast, you know! And then he or she will quarrel invariably with my little ones! No, I cannot take that risk! Sorry!" he started retreating into his house.

The client stood there puzzled and staring. Of course, he was desperate for a flat, but how on earth could he make a promise so unearthly! The chill in the air caught him squarely now.

"YOU ARE INVITED...!" (1)

We could see the activities down in the longish courtyard of our colony. The courtyard was surrounded by buildings divided into blocks on three sides with the front side having the main entrance gate. Comfortably seated in the portico of our third-floor flat, we often took a window view of the goings-on in the courtyard around the garden located in the center. This time, it looked like preparations for some social ceremony. Soon, we knew.

It was going to be the marriage ceremony of the colony Secretary's only son. We heard it not from the horse's mouth as yet, but from other neighbors. We knew the Secretary's family housed on the ground floor of the same block quite well; I was often talking to the Secretary on various issues including domestic ones while my wife was friendly with both him and his wife. So, we expected to be invited for sure. And, so it came.

One morning about three days before the marriage, I was as usual going through the daily newspapers, and my wife was busy in the kitchen making breakfast. The doorbell rang. Before I could free myself from my reading, my wife promptly trudged up from the kitchen and opened the door. The Secretary was standing in the doorway. I looked closely as I stood up to welcome him, and saw that he was carrying an envelope.

My wife cordially ushered him in, and we all sat down. He placed the envelope on the center table delicately and started the usual discourse on the background of the coming event. My wife was mostly talking and making sweet queries about the bride, her bio, family details and other bits of information. The neighbor was friendly enough, answering her while casting frequent looks at me. *Is he a little fidgety?* I wondered. *Why should he be?* It was all about a very happy and momentous occasion.

A little too suddenly, so I thought, the Secretary stood up and gestured to me picking up the cover from the table. I stood up, too, expecting to be invited formally. Looking, rather staring, at me fixedly, he opened the envelope taking out the invitation card. He handed it over to me in a grand formal style speaking slowly, "You please come. The reception starts in the evening. Please come…you." There was something odd about the 'you' he uttered. Very soon I found out why.

He left hurriedly afterward without even looking at the third person present there. My wife was sitting there all the time watching the invitation drama unfolding before her unbelieving eyes. Our Secretary-neighbor was apparently oblivious of her presence during that time. Closing the door behind him, I looked at my wife giving her a mischievous grin, "See, I'm privileged, the chosen one!"

She sank deeper into the cushiony comfort of the armchair putting her hands behind her head and laughed out loud. She kept on laughing for quite some time. I too heartily joined in the eerie merriment and said, "Do you happen to know of any constraint on our friend's budgetary allocations? Well, I'm wondering why these economy-class sentiments! On second thoughts, I'd rather not attend the wedding. I'd rather help him out on his austerity drive!"

"No…no! You must. We need not show our hurt or whatever to him and them at all. Our specific feelings on this matter are our own!" my wife said magnanimously.

However, as luck would have it, I could not attend the ceremony due to a work emergency on that day.

"YOU ARE INVITED...!" (2)

Deben was not surprised when his old colleague Bedanta called in the morning and desired to meet him. Bedanta told him sometime back that the marriage of his only daughter was coming up, and that Deben must be present. Bedanta was not just a colleague, but also a friend thanks to their long association in work. There were family-level interactions too at various opportunities. His daughter, a sweet child, was known to both Deben and his wife, Anjana. He already discussed it with Anjana to not miss that occasion, and buy a nice gift in advance. So, he said yes immediately, and informed his wife that Bedanta would be coming in the evening.

Deben decided not to take the afternoon nap that had become customary over the last few months after he retired from service. Particularly, after his road accident a month back that fractured his right hand, he was still burdened with the plastered right hand held in a strap.

The doorbell rang around six in the evening. As he stood up and opened the door, Anjana also joined him in the drawing room. Bedanta was ushered in. After an exchange of pleasantries and the courteous query about the progress of Deben's fractured hand, all of them sat down. Bedanta was carrying a colorful cover, which he delicately put on the table. Now, Deben was a little surprised or rather amused that Bedanta did not come to the point straightway, and instead, started a discussion on mundane office and pension matters. Anjana, in between, asked a few questions about family matters, which elicited answers that were a bit too prompt. *Is he trying to avoid her?* Deben thought. *But why?*

Anjana excused herself in the middle of the chatter and headed for the kitchen. She was not at all piqued or annoyed; as an ideal Indian homemaker, she went into the kitchen for the customary tea and snacks, this hospitality to guests being a traditional way of life. This kind of 'retreat' is very well understood by all kinds of guests and so well anticipated by them that they often intervene with, "No, no! Tea is not needed…sit…let's talk some more!" However, Bedanta did not offer any kind of intervention at her departure. Deben was also not at all perturbed, although a little piqued.

As if he were waiting for such kind of an opportunity, Bedanta stood up immediately, picked up the invitation letter, and offered to make a formal presentation. His amusement fast giving way to annoyance, Deben stood up too, reluctantly. Bedanta handed over the invitation muttering, "Please do come." Deben, formally receiving the letter, wanted to make light of the occasion saying, "What man! No formalities please, she is like our daughter…we will definitely be there…!" but he stopped short as his eyes went over the envelope.

Only his name was written on the cover. Neither his wife's name nor the add-on 'and family' was scribbled on the cover. He was not only surprised now but heartily shocked. *How could he?* Anjana knew his daughter even more closely than him. The budgetary compulsion of limiting guests did not quite apply to Bedanta because he earned a healthy retirement package recently, and it was his only child—the only marriage party to be celebrated ever in the family! With these thoughts racing through his mind, Deben still kept his air of nonchalance as he opened the envelope, took out the invitation card and commented how beautifully it was made.

They sat down and resumed their chatter; Deben with some reserve now. Anjana entered with a tray of tea and snacks. Deben tried his best not to have eye contact with her. Bedanta smiled at her as if nothing transpired in the meantime. Anjana fondly picked up the letter…and froze; she had the presence of mind to remain calm, however.

Immediately after Bedanta left, Anjana burst out, "What's this? That fellow never uttered a word to me! Not asked me to come even once!"

"Only I'm invited! Not you, darling! You already saw the invite!" Deben said sadly.

"That lousy miser…even then…how is it possible?" She fretted and expressed dismay. And suddenly she became calm, resigned. "Okay…no problem! Your friendship…you keep it…you attend!"

"Yes, I'll still have to go. And you'll have to accompany me!"

Anjana stared at him in disbelief.

"Are you out of your mind? You witnessed how that fellow insulted me! You have no respect for your wife… for your life partner?"

"I have, my dear! I'm as angered dismayed and irritated as you. But you know the kind of state I'm in now. I'm still an invalid. You must accompany me!"

"Your entreaties will have no impact on me! I'll never see his face again!"

The heated debate went on for a long time. At last, Anjana seemed to pity him for his 'friend', and his fractured self. She declared that she would accompany him on one condition: she would wait in the parked car with the driver for company till he came back. Deben knew it was his best option, and he accepted it.

On the appointed day, it happened as it was planned. Anjana dropped him at the wedding hall gate, asked the driver to park the car a little away, and waited in the car.

Deben tried to be his normal self at the party but was very hurt Bedanta never asked about Anjana even once. He got some solace seeing a whole lot of other males loitering around without their better halves.

There was a hiccup at the end. Deben said goodbye and tried to walk away too quickly. However, Bedanta insisted on seeing him to his car. Deben was shaken up imagining what would happen when Bedanta found a face in the car window glaring vengefully up at him! He couldn't afford to let it happen. "No, you cannot come…I mean you need not come…please attend to your other guests!"

Without allowing him to respond, Deben walked away, forcing even his fractured hand to swing freely.

THE DUEL

"Oh, you've come at last! I phoned you several times, you didn't bother to answer…okay, what did the doctor say? Has your little toe healed?"

"Actually, I had to sit there for nearly one hour; but the doctor hardly took any time. I walked out just after 7 p.m. I wanted to call you then but thought you must be on the way back home, and so decided to call later…actually, one of my friends lives nearby, she called me when I was waiting at the clinic; she invited me home. She came up to take me from the clinic. Their flat is nice and cozy…"

"That's fine…but what did the doctor say?"

"…not like ours—congested lanes and non-airy—homely locality. I was also feeling tired after a hectic day… she offered to make tea…"

"But what did the doctor say?"

"You're always impatient and rude! Just want to know what you want to know, quick and fast! All males are like that! Wait, I'll come to your point shortly…she made a very nice and tasty roll; I really enjoyed it with the tea, and relaxed. Meantime, her sister called from our native town. Actually, her sister lives just behind our ancestral house…I never knew that, and never met her there. My friend handed me the mobile to say hello to her. We talked a lot. You know, we last met in school days only…she married much before me and went from place to place with her husband's transfers. Now they've settled in our place…"

"Your friend lives so near to the clinic…so many times we went there, and she never invited us to their place…"

"Again, you're diverting the issue, I'm not talking about that, I'm telling you of my acquaintance with a lady after so many years. Next time we visit our native place, I'll definitely meet her…"

"What you say and do is always right. You see, I too need to speak my mind sometimes…but you hardly give me the opportunity, and get angry whenever I intervene. Okay, forget it, just tell me what the doctor said and advised."

"Now, you're starting it all over again! We can hardly discuss anything nowadays…we just land up with a bitter quarrel…"

"Nobody is quarreling now. I've not started anything; I only wanted to know what I needed to know…"

"I know… you'll never admit. You're always right! Fine, I'll not tell you anything now…"

"Damn it all! Tell me, why the heck I should listen to you talking about some lady I've never known or never met even after enjoying more than fifty beautiful springs of my life!"

"Then why at all you've come to talk to me?"

Thoroughly fed up, the husband stomped out of the room, resuming his television news watching in the living room. The wife, sprawling comfortably in the double bed, coldly opened the social media app in her mobile and got busy.

OUT OF THE CLUE

He was in an exuberant mood, full of positive energy, as he reached home that evening, got freshened up and settled down on the living room sofa; the day in the office being a very productive one. He wanted to lose no time sharing it with his wife. He called out to her; she was in the kitchen just putting the tea-pot on the gas burner while she arranged the plates on the tray, taking out bits and pieces of snacks for light refreshment before supper.

"Hey…do you hear me?"

"Yes, a bit louder!" the wife responded allowing the water, milk, tea powder, sugar and other ingredients to turn into a most desirable boil before being poured out.

"I told you…no…that we were going to launch a new project soon? Well…today we got going and had the first team meeting. The meeting went off extremely good; all the team members acknowledged me as the undisputed leader, you know!" he relished the feel of telling this to the person he loved and admired the most in his life.

"One minute, I'm coming, my leader!' she called out as she came into the living room, set the tray on the center table and took a seat herself, offering him a cup of tea and prodding him to take a neatly cut piece of the cake she made that day.

"Thanks… All the members of the team are excellent, a mix of old and brand-new," the husband took a sip, accepted the cake and went on excitedly. "Among the members, there is a new one, a girl who joined only recently, but got into the business perfectly…"

"New girl? Well, how's she, I mean, is she good-looking?"

"Oh yes. She's pretty and very young!"

"Ok, good for you!" she was getting into a mood to tease him.

"What do you mean 'good for me'?"

"Why, you always love to be surrounded by pretty girls, no? Whenever I visit you in office, I find you in such situations!"

"You know very well it is always job-oriented. I being the approving guy in the creative department, they have to come to me for the final say. You also know that boys or girls are not the issue; it's only work and its demands. Don't you ever notice the boys loitering around me on your visits? I'm always focused and a bit emotional too. If somebody does good work, I feel very excited. I end up hugging the boys very often. And, mind you, I do have enough good sense not to do so to the girls on similar occasions." He exhaled in a relaxed way now.

"Well, my dear gender-conscious leader! Maybe you are eager to tell me more about the new lassie on the block?"

"She's very smart, well-dressed and has an ability to pick up immediately. Not only does she have good looks but also has a polished way of speaking with a lot of good humor. You see, I had played a part in her selection, and for that, she's so grateful to me! The moment she entered my room for the meeting, she bowed, thanked me profusely and shook my hand continuously…"

She looked a bit annoyed now. "Then go and hug her first thing tomorrow morning."

He was surprised. *From what to what,* he mused. *Had he spoken too much about the girl?*

"You people are always biased. You cannot tolerate other women coming in your man's life, whatever way it happens." He uttered trying to justify his sense of offense and to suffocate the anger that was slowly growing in him.

"Bullshit! All males are like that! They want to brag about the women in their lives, and display horrendous intolerance at any attempt of elaborative analysis! I give you permission, okay, to hug all girls in your office from now onwards!" she was louder now.

"Do you think I am some kind of a leech? I always trust you with all my heart and you…?"

"Don't go on bragging and bragging…how great and noble you are…like all others in your family! Only I know…the problems I faced coming to your main house. All are so concentrated on publicizing how great they are!" the beginning of the shrill in her voice irritated him.

"Now you are digressing, and it's very deliberate, I know! Whatever is the way it happens, you'll finally come down on my people, targeting them unnecessarily! Your deeds, your reactions are always justified…whatever you prefer to say. And if I say something about your male friends, all hell…!"

"Damn my male friends. That's you, essentially! You cannot even tolerate my speaking to my old classmates!

Hypocrites, braggers' family…" she jerkily lifted herself from the chair moving away fast with her unfinished cup of tea.

He plonked his cup on the table nearly forcing the remaining tea to spill over the table. He could hear her making unnecessary noises in the kitchen handling the utensils while carrying on with her invectives against him and her in-laws. Evening spoiled, he failed today also as on so many other occasions to track the lurking danger correctly and to pre-empt it. He decided not to contribute anything more to the rants and leaned back dejectedly on the sofa.

Why the hell did I have to share it with my wife? There are so many things in the office or elsewhere that had better be relegated to oblivion rather than being described to others, particularly spouses, he thought. Few things were also going on in his mind. Why was he in such an exuberant mood and so eager to share it? Did the presence of pretty girls in the office actually have any impact on that exuberance? *I love good company,* he reasoned, *be it of any gender, and it's perfectly natural to love good company. When good company combines with a good job done, why not react positively to it?* he went on. However, a few strands of doubt still haunted his mind…! *Somehow,* he had to admit, *ladies do have some uncanny abilities to intuit or decipher some behavioral patterns or activities much more clearly than the males!*

In the meantime, his wife's rallies subsided and his mind still carried on with the introspection, although lazily.

Maybe he dozed off a little because he was not aware of his wife re-entering the room and occupying the chair. Her words ended his reverie.

"What kind of fish preparation would you like for supper?" she queried innocently.

He did not prefer to respond, resuming his gloomy silence, slumped on the sofa. She went on though.

"I took the raw fish out of the freezer in the afternoon. Maybe you'd like to have fried fish before dinner?" She now smiled switching on the television set.

That appealed to him immediately. He planned to watch a live soccer match later that night, and fried fish as an appetizer would be just fine. However, he still did not respond, happy that normalcy threatened to limp back in.

A CURIOUS CASE FOR DELAYS

I made a discovery of sorts recently! You know, we have certain likes and dislikes, and we have been traditionally used to having instant reactions concomitant on these. However, I found out that such likes and dislikes are sometimes specific to the prevailing situation or circumstances. Depending on the prevailing situation or circumstances, our traditional likes could very well convert into unconventional dislikes or our traditional irritation could translate into new-found pleasure. I do, of course, run the risk of suffering from naiveté as you all may know this or be experiencing such deferential distinctions. But somehow, I am hell-bent on propagating my discovery to one and all.

Our crucial keyword here is 'delay'. Almost always, delays cause irritation or dislikes, and fury in extreme cases. You hate when your train or flight is delayed; you hate waiting when somebody's train or flight is delayed; you hate to be kept waiting for a meeting; you wholeheartedly dislike latecomers in the office; you get furious when your spouse is late for an important occasion and so on. These are all traditional and accepted reactions. Now, I will proceed to my discovery straightway without saying anything more in this context, which could be revealing prematurely.

That evening I landed up with a lot of time to kill. I had to receive a friend at the airport at a bit of a late hour, and after office, I had nothing important to do. I didn't consider it wise to go home all the way and then come back again all the way to the airport. Going to a movie was ruled out because theaters were not in the vicinity of the airport and I didn't have that much time. And then, I was ravenously hungry too. In my earlier trips to the airport, I had observed a cozy nice little restaurant right opposite the arrival gates. Therefore, I decided on that; took a little bite, boarded a bus and went to the airport.

Surprisingly, the traffic that evening was not heavy, and when I arrived at the airport, I still had at least two hours to kill. I started thinking about what courses of food and beverages should be taken so that the time-killing got done appropriately as I entered the restaurant.

Meanwhile, I decided on a drink as the first course. I took a good seat and looked around the restaurant. There were not many customers at that point in time and none of them belonged to the noisy variety. With the air conditioners working fine, it was cool and comfortable. I was in.

I waited and waited with the menu wide open on my table. The waiters were moving around on errands not exactly related to the few customers available. However, I didn't even feel an itch of irritation as I relaxed and settled comfortably in my chair.

Finally, when one of the waiters came up to me, I ordered my drink but was told that was not available. After that, whatever item I happened to fix my taste buds on was either not available or not with the appropriate flavor I wanted. But I was not at all angry or irritated. I rather smiled at him and tried again with the menu. Eventually, I had to cancel my drink and settle for a snack of the waiter's choice.

After the delightful delay in placing an order, now I was in for a more appetizing delay in serving the order. I was too happy watching the people eating or drinking or idling or loitering around and also the television screen where a local news channel was trying to burst out of the mute mode. Curiously, everything seemed interesting to me despite now a vehemently protesting stomach. I sat there—bemused, but contented and happy as the minutes ticked by.

I enjoyed my dish immensely when it finally arrived and then ordered for a tea. There was another juicy delay until the hot beverage came. After I finished my tea, relishing it with lingeringly tender and deliciously spaced-out sips, I asked for the bill.

I never thought that it would be the longest regurgitating delay of all the delays. The waiters as usual moved around busily with their errands, never bothering about me. If I had moved out of the place quietly, nobody would have noticed. Such was the business that was going on. However, I did not at all dislike the restaurant nor was I irritated with the boys. Instead, I was beaming and merry.

As I finally settled my bill, I got a call from my friend. Yes, he had just landed. I congratulated myself, *Wow...what a perfectly timed time-killing!* However, somehow, I couldn't give a healthy tip to the boys, although I was not at all irritated or angry!

"BECAUSE I NEEDED TO BUY...!"

I got late in the office, but it was not a problem because I needed to buy a kilo of potatoes only, which was crucial for the dish I planned to cook that night.

It was late in the hot summer evening when I finally left the office. Across the road was the major metro railway junction in the big city. As I descended the final steps leading to the underground station platform, one train, in the direction I was to take, roared out. To my chagrin, it was an air-conditioned rake.

Commuting on the beleaguered city's metro, you needed a lot of luck to deserve an AC rake because it still abounded in non-AC rakes and, if you wanted the pleasure of paying a minimum five-buck for a metro ride, arguably the cheapest rate across the globe, you had to pay a price in terms of a lack of comfort and a consistently erratic time schedule. Also, once aboard the non-AC trains in the rush and crush, you had to witness the sliding doors making at least three attempts to shut under normal circumstances at almost every stop, and you had the unenviable option of cooling yourself with your own free-flowing sweat. Nobody really complained about this in here, because they preferred the joy of accessing every possible facility at its cheapest, and protested vehemently at the slightest indication of a metro-fare increase, or for that matter, any fare increase.

The next train was due in four minutes, but ten minutes elapsed and no train came. Three air-conditioned trains came in the meantime in the opposite direction, increasing my irritation. However, getting delayed further didn't really matter. Because I needed to buy a kilo of potatoes only, which was crucial for the dish I planned to cook that night.

Finally, one train came in my way and as feared, a non-AC one. And it was overloaded already with hordes of eager passengers waiting to barge in. I knew that the accumulated crowds in the next three stations would make it unbearable. So, I decided to wait and luckily got a platform seat.

The train time schedule or the related still didn't improve. After another long interval of time, one more non-AC train paddled in. I didn't budge from my seat, wisely. In the meantime, two more trains came in the opposite direction, again both air-conditioned. I began to seethe now, even though I needed to buy a kilo of potatoes only, which was crucial for the dish I planned to cook that night.

The next train for me was non-AC again, but it came a little early and it was less crowded. So, I took it. I managed a standing space for the 22-minute ride to my destination. If you must know, it cost me just ten bucks duly deducted from the smartcard.

As I alighted from my home station, I took in a view of the vegetable vendors lined up on one side of the station with their green assortments displayed on wooden raisers.

I needed to buy a kilo of potatoes only, which was crucial for the dish I planned to cook that night. So, I still had the distinct advantage of completing it in quick time. I selected a vendor who was entertaining a lone customer at that moment. I quickened my pace and occupied my position next to the lone customer before anybody else could come up. However, I had no idea about what was in store for me.

The vendor and the customer were somehow guided by some unwritten law of slow motion. The customer showed extreme delight in selecting very small portions of a variety of vegetables—250 grams of this, 300 grams of that, 200 grams of another, and so on. The vendor seemed to partake in this delightful game by weighing those with exemplary care and with classical perfection, putting the cuttings neatly into polyethylene bags of various sizes. The slow-motion show was aptly followed by the mandatory drama of accounting and budgeting as I still stood there. It was an elaborate process, even though the final budget turned to be much lesser than fifty bucks.

I sighed with relief that finally, the show was over. But then, the climax happened. The customer produced a five-hundred rupee note out of his pocket, for his just fifty-buck bill. Under normal circumstances, any vendor would have shown bitterness and irritation at this audacious gesture. But no, not this time. The vendor tenderly accepted the note, which in turn forced him to lay bare his ponderous box of the day's collections. Rummaging through his treasure for quite some time, he finally managed to settle the change. It was a befitting climax, well-deserved too. However, I wasn't too sure for whom, me or the duo.

It was thanks to my years of immense experience that I firmly stood through, and bought my kilo of potatoes from him only.

Because…what the heck! A late supper wasn't going to starve me to death in any case.

THE ROUGH CUT!

It was long overdue. The fact of the matter was that there was a problem in that very part of the anatomy that needed the action, which therefore had to be postponed indefinitely. A persistent heat-boil in a very wrongly-placed location continued to torment him for weeks.

Paban's wife had been complaining a lot about how he looked so horribly ruffled, the overgrowth flowing all around uncontrollably and so on. She understood his problem but looking at him in that state day after day she seemed to forget the unfortunate fact temporarily. Paban often explained to her, "Let me recover reasonably well first. Then I'll definitely complete the task. Rest assured." But, as is the way with wives, her taunts, despair continued unabated, and Paban accepted all in a natural magnanimity.

Paban also had a somewhat contrasting situation. A few of his friends always appreciated his looks in that state and exclaimed that he really looked very handsome. One of them even took a snap of Paban at a family event and displayed it proudly justifying his assertion. Paban also liked the way he looked. He showed the photo to his wife, but she remained expressionless. He was not at all surprised by her indifference.

One fine morning, Paban felt that finally that long-overdue action could well be carried out. So, he set out to the nearest salon, which was quite well kept and air-conditioned. Yes, it was his heady overgrowth that needed a cut, and the wicked boil in the middle of it healed, almost completely now. One of the young boys there made him sit in the empty spongy chair before the mirror and waited for his instructions.

Paban told him very clearly that the hair had much overgrown and due to the summer heat, he was facing lots of problems apart from losing control in setting it. So, he gave strong instructions to make it very short. "No need for styles or looks; just make it short."

The boy confirmed it again, and then set out with his operation. Paban expected the normal scissors to be used as on all earlier occasions. However, before he could foresee any lurking danger, the boy lifted the motored hair-cutting machine and applied it on the right side of his head. The machine whirred around his right ear, and he still had no inkling of anything serious. He was rather happy that the machine, used for the first time on his head, didn't at all scratch at the head skin.

Over with his right-side operation, the boy stopped and asked Paban to take a look at the mirror and sanction approval for the operation to be completed. Paban picked up his specs and looked at himself hopefully. He was in for a great shock. He never experienced such a tormenting sight in his entire hair-cutting history.

The machine almost cleaned him up on the right side, leaving, perhaps, only the scalp. He was furious; more so, because the boy was asking his approval only after completing the horrendous action. He calmed himself the next moment. *It was my instruction to make it very short,* he thought. How could the poor boy know what 'shortness' Paban exactly wanted? Then there was the overwhelming fact; with his right side shamefully bared, he couldn't possibly go for moderation on all other parts of the head.

"You have totally destroyed me, exposed all my gray hairs too. Why didn't you use the scissors? In all salons I visit, they always use those manual things only. Anyway, nothing can be done now, carry on, dear!" Paban said sadly. The boy justified the faster speed and efficiency of the electronic device, in his earnest defense.

When Paban returned home, his wife was out on some job. Seized with an almost vindictive desire, he very tenderly took a selfie showing his head prominently and sent it to her mobile phone. Prompt came her angry reply, "Why did you leave that much hair? You should've cleaned up completely! You birdie bald!"

As it happened, a few days later, Paban met his photographer friend concerning some work. His friend immediately expressed his shock and dismay at the sight presented by Paban. "How can you do this? No respect for appreciating friends? How heavenly you looked the other day…and now! My good God!"

Paban always had this dilemma regarding his haircuts. Some, prominently his wife and mother, never approved his long uncontrollable hair saying the overgrowth hid his beautiful face. While some friends, both male and female, always appreciated his hair, particularly when overgrown. Who is right and who is wrong, had been the eternal question in his mind. Once his wife made a caustic remark, "Don't believe your friends. They don't want you to look smart; they like to keep you looking like an ordinary nondescript person!"

Till that day, Paban didn't have an answer, affirmative or negative.

THE DISCERNING COMMUTER

He was not sure. He could never deny that he never wanted it. He needed it, particularly at times when he was stressed and tired. However, he was not at all sure what way he should act, in general.

Yes, Amlan considered himself a deserving candidate since he was fast approaching the life landmark. He was not there now, but it was not that far off either. And, most of the other candidates often showed a bullish attitude, which always made his will stronger.

The evening that day was very warm and humid. And to add to it, the rush hour lingered on somewhat late into the night. Amlan couldn't get a seat and had to retreat to the farthest corner of the metro train coach near the coupling. There he found some standing space with his briefcase tucked in between his legs. As he leaned against the side panel near the coupling opening, he watched quietly the movement around those seats that meant so much or so little for him. He was not sure, as usual.

The occupier at one of the two four-seat benches got up and that seat was vacant. The commuter nearest to the seat was a little balding but a younger man in his prime. The younger man looked greedily at the inviting seat but decided to check if genuine contenders were there or not. His looks finally settled on Amlan, and it became a lingering one, also furtive as if he were trying to find out Amlan's credentials, and at the same time, not wanting to let go.

Amlan didn't make any move because he was not sure. Apart from the fact his destination was just two stations away and that he was relatively comfortable in his present position, his continuing dilemma of so-near-yet-quite-far-off prevented him from going for the grab. He began to study the younger man with interest now.

From his uncertain looks, Amlan thought with certainty that he, in fact, found Amlan genuinely deserving, but did not want to give up on the windfall. Amlan's indecisiveness also emboldened him to go for it. Now Amlan felt offended because he thought the commuter was very close to being a bully. Therefore, finally, he made a move for it. But it was too late. Perhaps, sensing the impending probability of the near-senior citizen asserting his right, the apparently younger man occupied the seat in an instant dash, not bothering to look up at Amlan. The whole of that curious drama probably took less than ten seconds.

As always, Amlan couldn't suppress the grin trying to crack open his lips. The senior citizens enjoy two rows of seats at both ends of every coach of the metro railway rakes that also include the differently-abled, and it was always interesting to observe the mental wars between potential contenders. In India, one becomes a senior citizen after the age of sixty. However, from sixty to eighty plus years of age, one is still a senior citizen only, and so the deserving stamp of the contenders is always relative. Nobody could possibly tell or ask about the age and there was no way of verifying anybody's case because there is no system of checking identity cards or pension papers. Therefore, the relative gray intensity of the hair or the lack of it or the relative frailty of the body or the emaciated features were the only guidelines.

But whatever be the case, Amlan could not prevent himself from giving a rueful look at the young man, still seated securely and stiffly without looking around, as he alighted at his station.

THE DECIBELS OF DESPERATION

Tiken had developed a gut feeling. That he was not going to win this time. He tried hard to get rid of that miserable feeling but was not successful. He understood his other gut feeling too, that he cannot afford to lose this. He had everything to lose if he did. In fact, Tiken had sounded a threat even before the event that he would leave the place in case the inhabitants stopped supporting him, and they would miss his prestigious presence sorely. Then, he mused, *Did he actually know about the wave for change in the air? Perhaps yes, perhaps not.*

It was a huge high-rise housing society that Tiken lived in, with five wings from 'A' to 'E'. Each wing had around a hundred flats, most of which were occupied, either by owners or tenants. As the General Secretary of the Society's Residents' Association, he had been enjoying immense powers in taking decisions or initiatives or desirable actions. He was elected in the last elections by a very narrow margin, but most of the members in his executive committee won comfortably, and he was comforted by the total support extended to him by the members. It was his first time. He was propped up by his friends/associates as he was known to be a very influential person in the area with powerful contacts and links.

During his tenure, Tiken did many things right, like arranging for intercom facilities in every flat, full security staff in each wing, CCTV cameras in the passages and lobbies, robust events at every festive occasion with the presence of important ministers, increase in the hours of water supply, maintenance of a clean environment all around and so on.

He admitted that many of his other actions were misunderstood or the residents were misled by opportunistic agents, and these created a series of controversies and grumbling opposition. Like, he permitted a well-known grocery chain to establish a cooperative store inside the society complex and he prohibited the salesmen of quite a few other business firms from door-to-door marketing; he allowed his treasurer, his best buddy in every respect, to siphon off parts of the annual or occasional contributions of the residents regularly for personal use; and so on.

Tiken knew he was not dead right in taking those decisions. Actually, he could not say no to his dear friend, the treasurer, who had introduced him to this powerful post. The grocery store had been his treasurer's choice, and the treasurer promised him that the store, in utter gratification, would supply him quality products every month, totally free of cost. Again, he listened to his treasurer's advice to bar entry of random salespersons to the buildings, and instead, channelized entries from selected firms at a monthly fee of the proceeds of which were equitably shared between the executive members. He aggressively justified the personal use of public funds: well, every dedicated service must have a remuneration, at least for teas and refreshments.

Leaks of information always take place and discontentment spreads fast, he understood. However, he was sure he and his helpful associates could still have controlled the situation perfectly until the next elections. But the pandemic changed it all.

His every action during the cursed reign of the disease was hotly contested and opposed. First, he introduced a centralized agency for home-delivery of grocery and fruits, and disallowed households to order from their favorite local stores. They were also not allowed to combine in groups to select a particular online delivery chain.

Second, the powerful Secretary barred the entry of sweepers and car-cleaners to the society complex. This led to a pandemonium amid the pandemic: How would the presence of the cleaners jeopardize the health of residents as they would do their jobs outside and never even enter the building lobby? That this action would finally make the environment dirty and hazardous?

Third, the honorable Secretary never allowed health and free-testing camps inside the complex, saying that most of those health workers were bogus and useless, and they would in fact bring in the virus. In fact, he totally canceled the budget meant to be spent on health-related activities of the residents. This, again, led to widespread condemnation inside the society.

Tiken defended all these and other minor actions stoutly and said that the residents were all confounded fools, not understanding his altruistic concerns. In his poll campaigns, he asserted again and again that the society comes first, and given the support, he would transform this into a totally independent and self-reliant society. They should never listen to the distractors and the traitors, he shouted, the louder the nearer came the hour of the poll. To relieve his growing tension, Tiken announced his victory even before the counting began, which made even his treasurer warn him to tread cautiously.

The very first trends in the counting floored him. Only 'A' wing going in his favor; 'B' and 'C' gone and in 'D' and 'E' he was trailing at one and leading at another. He knew he could not afford to lose this election. He had everything to lose: he, possibly, would not be able to live there anymore, because, apart from all others, there had been a huge deficit in the annual budget, and without being in power, he won't be able to handle that. But, of course, he was certain that his devout supporters would continue to be there even if he lost, waiting for an opportunity to bring him back or establish his philosophy again.

With more ominous trends indicating the obvious, Tiken lost all self-control and caution. He started shouting, bickering, crying and monstering. "It's a fraud! My enemies have entered the offices! They're stealing my votes! Stop the counting! I'm going to the courts…I'll see you all!" His friends rushed in, but were no longer able to contain or calm him.

They try to reason with him, "Sir…how can you stop the counting without any sign of any wrongdoing? Courts or magistrates wouldn't listen to you either! Relax, and better go for a badminton match!"

"But why those scoundrels refuse to acknowledge? It's me who helped them vote through emails, it's me who helped even the ex-residents vote by postal ballots…in these tough times…and finally, they won't even support me!" he bellowed disconsolately.

Tiken suddenly took note of the street doggie sitting calmly on a sofa of his drawing room. Yes, he was such an ardent animal lover too! But nobody cared for his virtues! He hated that calm and composed rival of his, Biren! *No, you cannot win and enjoy my power by stealing it all,* he rants on. His roving eyes lock on the dog's again. A voice from inside his turmoiled epicenter called out, "Perhaps you could learn a few things from that dumb animal!" But in vain. Counting went on endlessly, his ire and venom showing no sign of ebbing…

THE BLOATED MUSICIAN

He had just two lousy obsessions in his artistic existential being. First, he believed firmly in what he said, "East or the West, I am the best!" Second, he always wanted others to tell him, hype him, move around him and worship him like an artist…nope…like the Hero!

He learned the classical method of playing his Indian instrument through a plethora of gurus so that he could finally perform on stage. With only a few stage performances, he ballooned into an ill-gotten pomposity thus creating a chain of ill-fated disciples and making quite a few ill-humored connections. Like you build your down lines!

He managed to capture several concerts outside India too through his connections that were desperate enough to help him have those to get rid of him permanently. Now, with his foreign trump cards, he started manufacturing more hype for himself.

When performing on stage, he was totally focused on the audience rather than on his music. Of course, he wanted his audience to applaud him, to hail him and never get the opportunity to look askance at him all through the musical act. When he observed that his accompanying artists had earned a few claps, the noble artiste never failed to give him/her a penetrating look saying, "Hey you! It's my solo, right? Better mind your own business!"

True and sincere to his nature, he was always chivalry incarnated when seeing ladies, or more specifically, foreign ladies around. His benevolent self never stopped him from announcing how great he was to the fairer beholders.

Once in an Indian small-town concert, he spotted an American lady in the auditorium lobby. Instantly in action, he went up and accosted her warmly.

"Hello, Milady! Welcome to India and to my music!"

"Oh, hi! You are performing tonight, right?"

"Yea, yea! Thanks a lot for coming! You see, only last month I performed in your great city!"

"Really? Was that good?"

"The response was damn good! But there was a small mishap!" He looked listlessly around.

"Oh? What happened?"

"Well, I lost my brand-new Mercedes Benz!" He announced with pride leaking through the whole of his existential being.

"Good heavens! How was that possible?"

"I don't know even now! That beautiful thing just vanished from the parking lot!"

"But your chauffeur should have been in the car, no?" The American lady looked puzzled.

He hardly knew what a 'chauffeur' meant. But he stuck on to his publicity stunts even as his unease started surfacing.

"You see, I just bought the car and wanted to drive it around myself considering the fact that I am damn good at that. I parked it and devoted myself to my music. After music, it was gone!"

"But of course, you claimed for insurance, right? However, you come to our country only for shows. How come you bought a car there? Astounding! Lost cars are always traced back quickly in the US. Very sorry to hear that."

The great musician was getting a little worried anxious and irritated now. How was he supposed to know the car purchase procedures in the US! Expecting more salvos, he frantically started looking for his next musical victim and luckily, he found one.

"Thanks for your concern, Milady! But you must excuse me now! See you there!" He nearly leaped away.

The American lady shrugged off into an amused resignation and headed toward the auditorium entrance.

Meantime, the great musician was already halfway into narrating another exotically concocted anecdote of his pristine existence.

THE THAMES POND
QUADRILOGY

1. CREDIT CONTROL ROOM

"Hello, this is Moneycanny. How can I help you, Sir?"

"This is Pond. Thames Pond. It's regarding my card accounts."

"Hello, Mr. Pond. I'll definitely answer your queries, but before that, please give a few details for our verification."

"…"

"Okay, thank you, Mr. Pond. Now please tell me."

"Well, Ms… err… you see. I've multiple credit card accounts with you a few of which I've been trying to close for over a year now. Every time they say my requests are being forwarded, but ultimately I get charged for annual fees for cards I've forgotten about."

"I'm sorry about that, Mr. Pond. But, Mr. Pond, the annual fees got waived every time."

"But I want them closed, canceled."

"I'll definitely forward your request, Mr. Pond. But, Sir, you are our esteemed customer and we get extremely sorry if people like you want to close your accounts."

"The problem is I don't need them. You can see that I've never used some of them for years."

"Mr. Pond, our credit cards are very powerful and have a lot of benefits. And you may need them in any kind of emergencies. So why not keep them, it's free too."

"But I don't need them. And I'm not a beggar to ask you for waivers again and again."

"Right, Mr. Pond. I'm making this... and that account... lifetime free. This I can do immediately online."

"But I don't..."

"Mr. Pond, you have an excellent track record with us and that's why we can do this for you. You are a special privileged customer. In fact, I've got a pre-approved Nut Credit offer for you."

"No. I'm not interested. You are not closing my dead accounts and on top of that you want to give me an additional credit card!"

"Nut Credit saves you huge amounts of money on everything—purchases, transactions, withdrawals, everything. Some are without service charges and totally free, Mr. Pond."

"No, I'm not interested."

"Nut Credit relieves you of the big burden of paying the high normal rate of interest month after month. It's on a daily basis and really hassles free."

"I'm not ..."

"Nut Credit also operates like any savings or current accounts, and so you enjoy all the associated benefits accordingly. This is an offer made just for customers like you, Mr. Pond."

"But I'm…"

"Nut Credit charges you only a nominal annual fee and a still smaller renewal fee every year. Mr. Pond, when you start getting the huge benefits, you'll really feel it's nothing."

"But…"

"Thank you, Mr. Pond. You'll get your new card in ten working days. Is there anything I can help you with, Sir?"

"Well…yes…no…but…"

"Thanks for calling, Mr. Pond. Have a great day."

2. THE COST OF CREDIT

"Hello! Mr. Pond?"

"This is Pond. Thames Pond."

"Good Morning, Mr. Pond. This is Moneycanny. Can I have two minutes of your time, please?"

"Regarding what?"

"Well, Sir, this is regarding a new revolutionary scheme meant only for privileged customers like you."

"I'm not really interested, but you can tell me in brief."

"Thank you for your patience, Mr. Pond. You see, today's times are very uncertain. Nobody knows what happens and when. In case of unfortunate demise or fatal accidents, our bank will protect you by waiving off all dues on your credit card plus an assured amount. All these for a nominal premium…"

"Well, Ms…err… look! This is a very fine morning and I'm out to work with a very fresh mind. Please don't spoil it with that talk of death and all!"

"Sorry about that, Mr. Pond. But this is a benefit with only minimal cost."

"What do you mean minimal? You just said I have to die to get the benefit!"

"Don't take it that way, Sir. You have a responsibility to your family. To your dearest wife."

"Look, my wife will be so grieved at my death that she will not be compensated at all by your money."

"But your children will definitely…"

"Not at all Ms. …err…, again! They will be equally grieved by my absence and they will try their best to prove their worth so that my soul rests in peace."

"Mr. Pond, this is a privileged offer meant only for customers like you. Our bank cares for you at every step of your life. And as I told you, this is at almost no cost."

"My death is a huge cost for me, you see? You want me to die and then benefit me! I don't want to die. Sorry!"

"No, Mr. Pond. We don't want you to die. We want you to live forever. I'm very sorry about your feelings."

"But…well…err… I see now how you fool…"

"Thank you, Mr. Pond. It's our great pleasure to enroll you in this unique scheme. Your next statement will reflect this change. Have a great day, Sir."

"Hey…Ms…err…wait a minute. I've not confirmed. Hello…on the contrary I've refused your offer. Hello… Damn it!" (Click-Crash)

3. CASH ON THE CARDS

Our friend Mr. Thames Pond often gets bogged down by his multiple credit card accounts. He tries to get rid of some now and then, but he gets into more traps and liabilities. On top of it, he gets bombarded with new and newer card offers. Due to his inability to refuse ladies, he succumbs to the baits cleverly set by the card executives. He is particularly scared of the wily executive called Moneycanny whose name he cannot even clearly pronounce. He is getting another call from her now. This time, he prepares to get bold with her...

"Hello!"

"Hello! Can I speak to Mr. Pond please?"

"This is Pond. Thames Pond."

"Good morning, Mr. Pond. This is Moneycanny. Can I have two minutes of your time, please?"

"Err...Ms...Regarding what?"

"Well, Sir, there is a special cashback offer for our most valued credit cardholders like you."

"Okay, tell me how do I get the cash?"

"The highest percentage cashback will be on your utility bill payments like telephone, mobile or electricity bills. This means you will regularly get some cashback every month. Then you will also get cashback on other transactions though at lower rates, but never less than one percent."

"But I do not want to make any payments."

"Sorry? You don't make any bill payments or pay for other purchases?"

"I mean I don't want to make any payment to you for this offer."

"Oh… Mr. Pond! There is no such payment involved in this offer."

"You mean to say I will keep on getting the cashback just like that!"

"Definitely, Sir, these are benefits for our privileged customers only. There is no annual fee and your lifetime free card is still valid with this offer."

"Are you sure? What about hidden costs?"

"Mr. Pond, I assure you there is absolutely no hidden cost."

"Okay then, I am game for some high cash!"

"Thanks, and congratulations, Mr. Pond. I am enrolling you in this offer. Our executive will confirm your status through a phone call within twenty-four hours. There is a one-time activation charge of a thousand bucks, which will reflect on your next month's credit card statement."

"I told you I am not going to make any payment to you for this offer. I asked you a thousand times about the charges. Now, what's this?"

"Sir, this is not a fee! Only an activation charge! Considering the cashbacks you are sure to get continually, this charge is just nothing."

"My dear Ms…err…whatever you'd like to call this. You are making me pay a thousand bucks and this will take me my lifetime to get that back through your cashbacks. Sorry, I told you. Take me out of it."

"Mr. Pond, please consider again. This offer ceases tomorrow."

"It ceases right now for me, milady! No payments please!"

"Thank you very much for your time, Mr. Pond. Have a good day."

"Thank you!" (click of phone disconnected) "Ha! Ha! Ha! Got you this time, baby! Hurray!"

4. THE VIRTUAL TRAVEL PACKAGE

Emboldened by his earlier encouraging experience with the banking hawks, Mr. Thames Pond decides to carry on from there. He takes a pledge to encounter any call from any credit card or banking executive with guts and intelligence. He must ensure that he refuse all unnecessary offers or entrapments. He'd no longer be vulnerable. And then, as usual, he gets a call right away...

"Hello...am I speaking to Thames Pond, please?"

"Who's this, please?"

"This is Moneycanny, Sir, from UC bank! Mr. Pond?"

"Right, this is Pond. Thames Pond!"

"So nice to talk to you again! Good morning, Sir!"

"Good morning. Ms. err...!"

"Mr. Pond...can I take just two minutes of your most precious time?"

"Regarding what?"

"Sir, you are one of our most privileged customers. We've reviewed your payment record over the years and found your credit history absolutely sound. Therefore, we'd like to offer you a rare privilege in terms of travel benefits. We are sending you a package of travel vouchers allowing you to have free five-star hotel comforts in various tourist locations you'd like to visit. We need your consent, Sir, so that we can forward that package to you readily."

"You are giving me all these free, milady?"

"Absolutely, Sir! This is our thanksgiving to one of our most privileged customers."

"No payment? No hidden costs? Are you sure?"

"Yes, Sir! All you have to do is to receive it!"

"Okay…in that case I can consider…Ms…err…!"

"Thanks, Sir! Your package is worth more than—bucks. So, there will be a service tax and other charges. You will pay an amount of—bucks for receiving the package. We'll bill this amount in your next card statement…"

"Hey…wait a minute! What are you saying…I'll have to pay to receive your benefits?"

"No, Sir! You are not making a payment; you are only paying taxes. Your package is worth a lot of money and so service charges apply naturally…"

"Wait a minute…you see…"

"Ours is one of the largest banks of the country with a huge network…"

"Hey…Ms…err…I'm not referring to your bank…I mean you see…that is 'you'…and 'see'… here! You see… err…you…see…I will have to take leave from my office… book tickets…plan it perfectly to be able to avail of your travel package, right? And considering your five-star privileges, I must travel by air…I cannot just crawl and slog to land up there, no? All, at my cost! Now, the problem is it may not materialize in that specified period of yours…due to so many reasons…!"

"But, Sir, we expect you definitely won't let go of such a money-saving opportunity!"

"Okay…you expect…I want to. But it is not in my hands. Now, if I fail to avail of your 'free' package, why on earth should I pay you in advance? You send it…I'll see, and then, if I do travel and enjoy your five-star luxuries, please bill the service charge…this makes perfect sense."

"Sorry, Sir! We offer you a value package and therefore we have to charge the service tax. Please confirm your agreement so that we can send it across immediately."

"I'm sorry too…milady! I cannot give my consent…" (Cuts the line.)

Mr. Pond watches his phone ring again. He rejects the call, deliriously happy. The process repeats itself one more time. Then silence as Mr. Pond indulges himself a broad grin.

Printed in Great Britain
by Amazon

23396453R00085